Something Wicked

Something Wicked

Scottish Crime Fiction

Edited by Susie Maguire
and Amanda Hargreaves

Polygon

Polygon
An imprint of Edinburgh University Press Ltd
22 George Square, Edinburgh

Reprinted 2000

Typeset in Minion by Hewer Text Ltd, Edinburgh, and
Printed and bound in Great Britain by
Bell and Bain Ltd, Glasgow

A CIP record for this book is
available from the British Library

ISBN 0 7486 6253 7 (paperback)

The Publisher acknowledges subsidy from

THE SCOTTISH ARTS COUNCIL

towards the publication of this volume.

Contents

Introduction

By Amanda Hargreaves

Maguire stared uncomprehending at the monitor screen. The library reading room seemed suddenly to have fallen silent. The soft rasping of fingers on paper had been replaced by a faint buzzing in her head. Hands shaking slightly, she hit the DELETE SEARCH key and typed in the three words one more time: Scottish; Crime; Collection. As she pressed ENTER she closed her eyes and counted 1, 2, 3 – the time it would take for the computer to display the search results. When she snapped them open, there it was again: the unbelievable NO TITLES FOUND. The back of her neck prickled and she felt herself grow cold with excitement. This was what she had been looking for: a chance to legitimise her habit. All she needed now was an accomplice – a

partner in crime. Hargreaves? Yes! Pulling on her fake fur jacket she hurried
out into the dark blustery Summer's day and headed with purposeful steps
along George IV Bridge, in the direction of George Square, the home of
Polygon Press.

And so it all began, the painstaking amassing of suspects, the doorstepping,
the phone calls at unsociable hours. Many's the night I've cursed that siren
song which lured me from the known parameters of my daily toil and into
the dangerous territory of editing a collection. I found myself entering a
twilight world of half-truths, of dark passions and of tough deals. With
Susie's elbow always sharp in my ribs, I relinquished any last hope of
leisure time. We tracked our prey up and down the country. We rudely
disturbed them in the midst of their secret lives, exploding with our own
enthusiasm and deaf to their pleas for extended deadlines, realistic
financial incentives and chocolate. Hardened by the grim reality of the
editing process – not so much champagne, Prada handbags and limousines
to ferry us about the country, more nasty decaffeinated coffee, inadequate
word processors and irascible bus drivers – we wheedled and bullied until
our ravening hunger for crime stories was satisfied.

Agatha Christie, Ngaio Marsh and Michael Innes paperbacks, discovered in the backs of bookcases in other people's houses, were the
endorphins that led to my own addiction. I grew up in the mistaken
assumption that 'Heaven' would be working on, with and around books. I
was therefore positively starry-eyed when I landed my first job – for a
London publisher. Moving South was a small price to pay, I thought, for
the chance to wallow in literature for ever. It didn't take me long to realise
that I had sentenced myself to a life of reading for work. On the surface this
does not sound too terrible – after all, any excuse to read will do – but in
reality it meant reading what other people told me to. This scarcely left any
time at all for reading for pleasure. I took drastic measures and pared
down my extra-curricular reading necessities to the barest essentials,
which consisted almost entirely of crime. By then I was aware that the
best crime novels are not *whodunnits* or *howdunits*, though they are still
usually *whydunnits*; we addicts are not merely attracted to a comfortable
escape from the dreariness of wet Sundays, long journeys and occasional
bouts of flu. Don't we all know the vicarious thrill to be had from those
sobering glimpses into other people's nightmares, the guilty pleasure of

watching safely from the sidelines? The ancient Roman public enjoyed the spectacle of gladiators slaughtering each other and in this kinder age we read crime fiction with the same relish. More often than not, though, we are attracted to the realism of crime fiction, to the characters we can identify with, to the places we know. It is no accident that the setting of a crime novel has become increasingly important. We want the action to be close to home and we want to feel that we are in some way ourselves involved. Coming back to Edinburgh to work for the BBC, I realised that Scotland had become a breeding ground for crime fiction of the best and purest quality. On my doorstep. I licked my chops and sharpened my teeth with anticipation.

But soon I wanted more, and here was my chance. The dictionary definition was generous: 'Grave offence punishable by law; evil act; such acts collectively; shameful act'. Such a bandwidth gave us licence to ask a broad cross-section of writers to apply themselves to the genre. Some were committed to other projects, some were not to be tempted, others found this an exciting challenge, and a number were seasoned professionals in the crime game. Most became enthusiastic. Beyond suggesting that there was no obligation to feature a body in the library or a maverick detective, we left the choice of crime entirely up to the authors.

The resulting collection contains unique interpretations, varying from incorrect social etiquette through to murder, taking in stalking, burglary, shop-lifting, intimidation, genocide, torture, theft, date-rape, feminist revenge, paeodophilia, the horrors of childhood and the fickle finger of fate. Some stories are serious, some darkly humorous. They are all wrought from the minds of apparently pleasant, sane human beings you might meet at the supermarket, in a café, down a dark alley any night of the week – and we hope you like them.

Amanda Hargreaves and Susie Maguire
March 1999, Edinburgh
With grateful thanks to Martin Corley for finding us a title

Bampot Central

By Christopher Brookmyre

There was a six-foot iguana swaying purposefully into Parlabane's path as he walked down High Street. It had spotted him a few yards back and instinctively homed in on its prey, recognising that look in his eye and reacting without mercy. Some kind of sixth sense told cats which person in any given room most detested or was allergic to their species, so that they knew precisely whose lap to leap upon. A similar prescience had been visited upon spoilt Oxbridge undergrad hoorays in stupid costumes dispensing flyers for their dismal plays and revues. It was for this reason that a phenomenon such as the Fringe could never have thrived in Glasgow. In Edinburgh, most locals were stoically, if wearily, tolerant of such impositions; though in the West, dressing up as a giant lizard and deliberately getting in people's way would constitute reckless endangerment of the self.

'There's no getting past me, I'm afraid!' the iguana chirped brightly in a stagy, let's-be-friends, happy-cheery, go on, please stab me, you know it'll make you feel better tone of voice. 'Not without taking one of these!' it continued, thrusting a handful of leaflets at him.

Parlabane had put on the wrong T-shirt that morning, forgetting that his errands would unavoidably take him through places residents knew well to avoid during the Festival (or to give it its full name in the native tongue, the Fucking Festival). He was wearing a plain white one, which was nice enough but vitally lacked the legend 'FUCK OFF – I LIVE HERE', as was borne on several others at home. His August wardrobe, he liked to call it.

'Keeble Kollege Krazees present: Whoops Checkov!' the leaflet announced. 'A hilarious pastiche of Russian Naturalism! Find out what Constantine really got up to with that seagull!' Followed by the standard litany of made-up newspaper quotes.

'Come along tonight,' solicited the iguana. 'It might even cheer you up a bit!'

Parlabane swallowed back a multitude of ripostes and summoned up further admirable self-control by keeping his hands and feet to himself also. He breathed in, accepted a flyer and walked on. Remain calm, he told himself. He was over the worst of it now, having passed the Fringe Society office. North Bridge was in sight.

It was his friend's son's birthday the next week, and the gift Parlabane wanted to get him was only on sale in a small toy shop on the High Street. If it had also been on sale at the end of a tunnel of shite and broken glass, he'd have had to think long and hard about which store to visit during this time of year; as it was he'd had no such choice. The gift was a posable male doll in a miniature Celtic kilt. The intended recipient lived in Los Angeles and would have no inkling of there being any significance to the costume, knowing only from Parlabane's attached note that the doll was to be named Paranoid Tim and must be subjected to every kind of abuse David's little mind could dream up.

He looked down at the pavement, carpeted as it was in further leaflet-litter, mostly advertising stand-up gigs by the A-list London safe-comedy collective, the ones who had each been bland enough to get their own Friday night series on Channel Four. He wondered whether anyone doing stand-up these days wasn't 'a comedy genius', and daydreamed yet again about Bill Hicks riding back into town on a black stallion and driving these lager-ad auditions into the Forth to drown.

Maybe he should have just sent the kid a card and a cheque, he thought, eyeing a nearby mime with murderous intent. But what the hell, he'd bought it now, and whatever he sent wouldn't spare him the next ordeal he had to face that day: a trip to the Post Office.

He picked up pace going down towards Princes Street, as the unpredictable crosswinds made North Bridge an inadvisable pitch for leafleting. The route was therefore comparatively free of obstacles, save for a gaggle of squawking Italian tourists staging some kind of sit-in protest at a bus-stop. Parlabane approached the St James shopping centre with a striding, let's-get-this-over-with gait, all the while attempting to take his mind off the coming horrors with another calming fantasy involving the three female flatmates from 'Friends'. This time he was disembowelling them with a broadsword, the chainsaw decapitations having grown a little tired.

It was too simplistic to lay the blame at the feet of the Tories' 'Care in the Community' policy. There had to be something deeper, to do with tides, leylines and lunar cycles, that explained why every large Post Office functioned as an urban bampot magnet, to which the deranged couldn't help but gravitate. From the merely befuddled to the malevolently sociopathic, they journeyed entranced each day, as though hypnotically drawn by the digitised queuing system. Parlabane remembered those Les Dawson ads a few years back: 'It's amazing what you can pick up at the Post Office.' Yeah. Like rabies. Or maybe anthrax.

He bought a self-assembly packing box at the stationery counter, then after ten minutes of being humiliated by an inert piece of cardboard, returned to purchase a roll of Sellotape and wrapped it noisily around the whole arrangement until Paranoid Tim was securely imprisoned. It looked bugger-all like a box, but the wee plastic bastard wasn't going to fall out, which was the main thing.

Then he joined the queue.

There were three English crusties immediately ahead of him, each boasting an ecologically diverse range of flora and fauna in their tangled dreads. They were accompanied by the statutory skinny dog on a string, and were sharing round a jumbo plastic bottle of Tesco own-brand cider and a damp-looking dowt. The dog wasn't offered a drag, but it looked like it had smoked a few in its time and probably preferred untipped anyway.

Behind him there was a heavily pregnant young woman, looking tired and fanning herself with the brown envelope she was planning to post. And behind her were a couple of Morningside Ladies muttering about whichever Fringe show had been singled out for moral opprobrium (and a resultant box office boost) this year by Conservative Councillor Moira Knox. He'd got off lightly, in other words, and the queue wasn't even very long. The ordeal was almost over.

Except that at the Post Office, it's never over till it's over.

He caught a glimpse of a figure passing by on his right-hand side, skipping the queue and making directly for the counter. Parlabane was following the golden rule of PO survival – never look anyone in the face – but was none the less able to make out that the person was wearing a balaclava. His heart sank. It was the number one fashion accessory of the top-level numpties, especially in the height of Summer, and this one looked hell-bent on maximum disruption.

Then from a few feet behind him he heard an explosion, and turned around to see fragments of ceiling tiles rain down upon the betweeded Morningsiders. Behind them was a man in a ski-mask holding a shotgun.

'RIGHT, NAE CUNT MOVE – THIS IS A ROBBERY!'

Parlabane turned again and saw that the balaclavaed figure at the counter was also holding a weapon.

Screams erupted as the people milling around the greetings cards and stationery section at the back animatedly ignored the gunman's entreaty and began pouring out through the swing-doors.

'I SAYS NAE CUNT MOVE!' he insisted, discharging another shot into the tiles, this time covering himself in polystyrene and plaster-dust. He wiped at his eyes with one hand and waved the shotgun with the other, running to the door to finally cut off the stream of evacuees.

'Lock the fuckin' door, Tommy, for fuck's sake,' ordered the balaclava at the front counter.

'I'm daein' it, I'm daein' it,' he screeched back. 'An' dinnae use and fuckin' name, Jyzer, ya fuckin' tube, ye.'

'Well whit ye cawin' me mine for, ya stupit cunt?'

Jesus Christ, thought Parlabane, watching the gunman on door-duty usher his captives back into the body of the kirk. It was true after all: the spirit of the Fringe affects the whole city. The worthy ethos of amateurism and improvisation had extended to armed robbery. Must have been Open Mic Night down at the local Nutters & Cutters, and first prize was lead role in a new performance-art version of *Dog Day Afternoon*.

From the voices he could tell they were young; but even if they had remained silent it still wouldn't have stretched his journalistic interpretative powers to deduce that they were pitifully inexperienced.

He rewound the action in his head, doing his Billy McNeil replay summary. Three seconds in, Mistake Number One: Discharging a shotgun into the ceiling to get everyone's attention, like simply the sight of the thing wasn't going to raise any eyebrows. There were several hundred people outside in the shopping mall, and a large police station 200 yards away at the top of Leith Walk.

Four seconds in, Mistake Number Two: Charging into the shop and leaving umpteen customers behind you, out of sight, with a clear exit out the front door, through which they rush in a hysterical panic.

Seven seconds in, Mistake Number Three: Blowing another hole in the roof, then turning your back on the remaining customers while you chase after extra hostages that you won't need.

Eight seconds in, Mistake Number Four: Telling everybody your first names.

Ten seconds in, Mistake Number Five: Finding yourself with at least ten customers plus staff as prisoners. One or two is usually plenty.

In a moment of inspiration, gunman Tommy began rearranging the queuing cordons and ordered everyone behind the rope.

'Stay there an' dinnae move, right?'

The customers were uniformly terrified, with the exception of Parlabane, who was just in far too bad a mood to entertain any emotions other than fury and hatred. Decadence is often born of boredom, nihilism even more often born of a walk through the Old Town in mid-August.

'Wouldn't you prefer us to sit down?' he offered, figuring these guys were going to need all the help and advice they could get.

Tommy thought about it. He looked like he'd need to do his working on a separate sheet of paper, but he got there eventually.

'Eh, aye.'

Jyzer was busy making Mistake Number Six: Pointing his weapon at a young teller and ordering her colleagues to stay in their seats, where they could each press their panic buttons just in case the two resounding shotgun blasts hadn't been heard first-hand at Gayfield Square polis emporium.

'Jesus Christ,' Parlabane sighed, the words slipping out before he could stop himself.

'Shut it, you,' Tommy barked. 'You got a problem, pal?'

Yes, he did. He had a problem with the fact that the chances of these two eejits shooting someone through incompetence-generated panic were increasing by the second. He considered amelioration the wisest policy right then.

'Eh, no problem,' he said. 'But I was wondering. . . . I mean, it's just an idea really, but maybe you should move the staff over here beside us, you know, so there's just one group of hostages to keep an eye on, and your china can get on with posting his airmail or whatever.'

'Christ, mate,' said one of the crusties, 'why don't you offer them our bloody wallets as well while you're at it? I mean whose side are you on?'

'Fuckin' shut it, you,' snapped Tommy. 'An' it's no airmail, it's a fuckin' robbery, right?'

Parlabane held his hands up and shrugged. Whatever.

Jyzer, who by superiority of one synapse was the brains of the outfit, had cottoned on to Parlabane's thinking and gestured the other tellers to file out from behind the counter. Then he ordered Tommy to collect everybody's wallets, proving that he was broad-minded and open to suggestions from any of the hostages.

'Sheer fuckin' genius,' Parlabane muttered to the crusty, who wouldn't meet his gaze.

Tommy backed away, eyes flitting back and forth between the growing pile of wallets and purses and the front doors, outside which a crowd had gathered.

'Oh, I just knew something like this was going to happen,' muttered one of the Morningsiders to her companion. 'I just knew it.'

'Me too, Morag, me too.'

Parlabane had suffered enough.

'Well, it's a pity neither of you fucking clairvoyants thought to tip anyone off, then, isn't it?' he observed.

'Now, son, there's no need for that.'

He looked away. This was the quintessence of British 'respectability'. There were two brainless arseholes holding them prisoner with shotguns, but they could still get upset about the 'language' you used.

Jyzer's initially quiet dialogue with the remaining teller was beginning to gain in volume. Parlabane hadn't caught what Jyzer was asking for, but he wished to hell the stupid lassie would hurry up and give him it, especially as there were now two uniformed plods peering in the doors and hustling the onlookers back. He looked at his watch, figuring the Balaclava Brothers had a few more minutes before an Armed Response Unit showed up to raise the stakes.

'Look, I ken ye're lyin, awright? We've had information. We ken they're in there. Insurance bonds, fae Scottish Widows. They come through here the last Monday o' every month. So fuckin' get them or I'll fuckin' blow ye away.'

The girl had tears in her eyes and was struggling to keep her voice steady. 'I swear to God, I've never heard of any . . . insurance bonds coming through here. In fact, I don't think I've ever heard of insurance bonds, full stop.'

'Look, don't gie's it. Last Monday o' every month. Scottish Widows. It should say it on the parcel.'

'But this isn't a sorting office. The only parcels coming through here are the ones folk are sending. They go straight in the slots over there, or in the basket through-by. Please, I'm not lying. You can come through and look.'

'I fuckin' will an' aw,' he said, walking around to the counter's access door. 'An' if ye're lyin' I'll fuckin' mark ye, hen. I'll no be a minute, Tommy,' he assured.

'Insurance bonds?' one of the tellers asked of a colleague.

'Naw, I've never heard of them either.'

'Wouldnae come through here anyway, would they?' queried another. 'D'you think they've got the right place?'

'Fuckin' shut it yous,' Tommy ordered again. 'We've had information. We ken whit we're daein' so sit nice an' it'll aw be by wi' soon, right?'

Parlabane sighed again. Insurance bonds. Jesus Christ Almighty. It just got better and better.

'What's an insurance bond, Tommy?' he asked calmly.

'I tell't yous aw tae shut it. I ken whit insurance bond's are, right?'

Parlabane made a zipping gesture across his mouth. There was a suspicion growing inside his head. It had germinated early on in the proceedings, but the last few moments had poured on the Baby Bio and it was seriously starting to sprout.

They sat in silence, apart from the occasional yelp from the crusties' skinny dog. Tommy's eyes looked wide and jumpy through the holes in his ski-mask.

'Fuck!' came a furious, low growl from the back office. 'Fuckin' Jesus fuckin' *fuck*!'

The girl stumbled nervously out to join the hostage party, followed by Jyzer, whose woolly mask could not conceal that he was little at peace with himself.

'So, d'ye get them?' Tommy asked.

Jyzer took a slow breath to calm his rage. It didn't quite make it.

'Naw, I never fuckin' got them, ya stupit cunt. Fuckin' Scottish Widows must've changed the delivery day or somethin'.'

'Aye, awright, dinnae take it oot on me.'

'Well, stop askin' fuckin' stupit questions.'

'But what are we gaunny dae?'

'Shut up, I'm tryin' tae think.'

Parlabane looked to the front of the Post Office. One of the uniforms was pointing in and talking to someone out of sight down the mall. Three men in matching kevlar semmits filed into place in front of the sports shop opposite, taking up crouching positions and raising automatic rifles.

Parlabane swallowed. Not everyone was going to be home in time for tea, he feared.

'Giros!' Jyzer announced. He turned to the teller who had most recently joined the ranks of the illegally detained. 'Giro money. Pensions nawrat. Hand it ower.'

'I don't think that should be your number one priority right now,' Parlabane said, pointing at the front window.

'Who asked . . . aw fuck.' Jyzer took a step back, like that extra two feet would put him out of a bullet's projectile range.

'This is the police,' announced a hailer-enhanced screech. Whatever it said next was lost as Jyzer finally showed a spark of dynamism.

'Right,' he stated. 'Staun up, aw yous. An' line up across the shoap, facin' away fae the windae. That's it.'

They got to their feet unsteadily, most of them turning their heads to cast an eye upon the assembly outside. Jyzer and Tommy stepped behind their human shield, out of the police marksmen's sights.

'Terrific,' muttered one of the crusties. 'Now we're the filling in a gun sandwich.'

'Noo, go an' get us aw the cash in the shop,' he commanded the teller, handing her the sports bag that already contained their wallet harvest.

'We have all exists covered,' resumed the loud hailer. 'Please put down your weapons, release your hostages and come out with your hands on your heads.'

'Come on,' said Parlabane tiredly. 'Do what the man asked. He said please, after all.'

'You think we're fuckin' stupit, don't ye?' Jyzer observed, accurately. 'Smart-arsed cunt,' he added, hitting a second bull's-eye.

'Well, maybe you'll prove me wrong by explaining how you were ever planning to get out of here, with or without your, ahem, insurance bonds.'

'Stop windin' him up, mate,' warned the crusty who had earlier proffered the highly constructive wallet suggestion.

'I'm not winding him up. I'm just curious to know the secrets of how true professionals work.'

'Want me tae slap the cunt, Jyzer?' Tommy offered.

'Just keep the heid and keep your hauns on the gun, Tommy. Dinnae let him distract ye. He's up to somethin', this cunt.'

A telephone started ringing on the other side of the counter as the teller returned with the sports bag, presumably now containing cash and very possibly a dye-charge, seeing as Jyzer had made Mistake Number Fuck-knows by leaving her alone to fill the thing.

'Get that,' Jyzer commanded. 'No you,' he added, as Tommy made to reach for the receiver.

'It's for you,' she said. 'The police.'

He gestured to her to rejoin the human shield, taking hold of the bag as she passed, then picked up the phone. Tommy stayed in place, sweeping the gun back and forth along his line of vision like it was a searchlight. The crusties' skinny dog ambled lazily over to him, yawned once and began half-heartedly shagging his leg.

'Get tae fuck, ya wee shite,' he hissed, kicking out at it to shake the thing off, his eye relaying between his prisoners and his foot. 'Fuckin' dirty wee bastard.'

'TOMMY!' Jyzer barked, placing a hand over the mouthpiece, 'will ye fuckin' keep it doon – I'm on the phone here.'

'Aye, awright. Fuck's sake,' whined Tommy, hurt.

Jyzer shook his head and took his hand off the blue plastic.

'Sorry, what were ye sayin'?' he resumed. 'Naw, naw. You listen. Fuckin' just shut it an' listen, ya polis cunt.'

The Morningside contingent tutted in stereo either side of Parlabane.

'Before we even have this conversation, I want to be lookin' oot that front windae an' seein' *nae* polis, right. Nane. Get them away fae the front o' the shop then phone us back.' He slammed down the handset with an obvious satisfaction. Parlabane suspected the sense of accomplishment would be short-lived, but was admittedly impressed at this first sign of Jyzer having any idea what he was doing. In fact, he had noted with some surprise that neither of the pair had shown much sign of panic at the arrival of the ARU, and started to wonder whether their grossly conspicuous entrance had been less of an obvious blunder than he had first assumed.

Jesus, these heid-the-baws couldn't have a *plan*, could they?

He looked back over his shoulder, Jyzer and Tommy peering between the arrayed hostages. The marksmen got to their feet and moved out of sight left and right, as if exiting a stage. Parlabane figured it a safe bet they'd be returning for the fifth act.

The phone rang again.

'Right. Very good. Well done. Noo here's what we want. Naw, naw, shut it. We aw ken what *you* want; you want the hostages oot an' us in the cells so's ye can boot fuck oot us. Well, the bad news is you cannae have baith, right? So there's gaunny have to be a wee compromise. You can have maist o' the hostages in exchange for a helicopter. We want it on the roof o' the St James Centre in hauf an 'oor. We'll be takin' wan hostage wi' us, an' we'll tell the pilot where we're gaun wance we're on board.' He slammed the phone down again.

'A helicopter?' Parlabane asked. 'What, has Fife no' got an extradition treaty?'

'Fuckin' shut it.'

'Another rapier-like come-back.'

'Right,' Jyzer declared, suddenly pointing his shotgun at the pregnant woman. 'Step forward missus, ye're comin' wi us.'

'No her, Jyzer,' Tommy dissented. 'She's dead fat. She'll be slow.'

'She's no fat, she's fuckin' pregnant, ya n'arse. The polis'll no mess aboot if we've got a gun tae a pregnant burd's heid.'

The pregnant woman began to whimper, tears running from terrified eyes. She put a hand out and grabbed Parlabane's shoulder to steady herself.

'Not a good idea, guys,' he stated.

The phone began ringing again.

'I thought I tell't you tae shut it,' Jyzer said, thrusting the gun into Parlabane's face.

'Look at her,' he demanded, staring into Jyzer's eyes. 'She's ready to burst. Do you want her goin' into labour during your dramatic getaway?'

Jyzer looked at the woman, sweating, tearful and imposingly up the stick.

'Know somethin'?' he declared. 'You're absolutely right. We'll take you instead.'

Parlabane, who was firmly of the belief that no good deed ever goes unpunished, had been expecting this. He shrugged, put his parcel down and took a step forward, trying not to dwell on the potential indignity of surviving several professional attempts on his life only to be plugged by some shambolic half-wit down the Post Office.

Bugger it. Just as long as getting killed there didn't mean you went to Post Office Hell.

Jyzer picked up the phone again while Tommy gestured Parlabane to walk ahead of him through to the area behind the counters. The skinny dog gave another yawn as they passed, then trotted over to Jyzer and began humping his shin, its pink tongue lolling out of the right-hand side of its mouth.

'Naw, naw. We'll let the last hostage go wance we've arrived at AYIAH! Get tae fuck, ya clatty wee cunt . . . naw, no you, officer. Dug was tryin' tae shag me leg.'

Jyzer eyed the crusty who was holding the other end of the string. 'Heh, Swampy, that thing touches me again an' I splatter its baws aw ower this flair, awright? Naw, no you officer. Aye, that's right, *aw* the hostages. Once we're up an' away, we cannae shoot them, right? So they're aw yours – but no' until we're up an' away. An' we're no comin' up until the chopper's there. If we come up the stairs an' there's fuck-all, it's gaunny be a fuckin' bloodbath, right? Cause ye'll no have gie'd us any choices – we'll have to shoot oor way oot. Noo, next time this phone rings it better be tae say wur transport's arrived?'

He put the phone down again.

'Are we gettin' a helicopter, Jyzer?' Tommy asked.

'Don't be a fuckin' eejit, Tommy. They're just stringin' us alang, same as we're stringin' them alang. C'mon.'

They backed into the passage leading to behind the counters. Tommy keeping a gun on Parlabane, Jyzer still training his on the hostages.

'Nane o' yous move,' he called out, stopping at the door that led into the storeroom at the rear of the counters. 'We'll be watchin'. Stay where yous are. You might no' see us, but we'll still see you. Dinnae try anythin'. Just cause ye cannae see us doesnae mean we're no there.'

'I'm sure they bought that,' Parlabane said, nodding, as they retreated into the store-room. 'I don't think it would have crossed their minds at all that you might not be watching them. I mean, if you'd overstated your case it might have raised suspicions, but . . .'

'Fuckin' shut it,' grunted Jyzer, nicking back and popping his head round the door to check his prisoners weren't making a swift but orderly exit.

'More Wildean badinage. Do you mind if I write some of these comebacks down?'

'You'll no' sound so smart talkin' through a burst nose, smart cunt, so I'd fuckin' wrap it if I was you.'

'And if you burst my nose you'll be leaving a nice fresh trail of blood along your escape route; that's if you fuckin' clowns have got an escape route.'

'We've got mair ay a plan than *you* think, smart cunt.'

'Course you have. You're fuckin' professionals. Tell me again about these insurance bonds . . .'

Jyzer back-handed Parlabane across the jaw, which was very much what he'd been hoping for. Unfortunately the blow came on the wrong side, so he had to execute a largely unconvincing 180-degree stumble before getting to his intended effect, which was to fall down heavily against the door so that it slammed loudly with his back propped hard against it.

Despite Parlabane's abysmally obvious pirouette, it still took Jyzer a few moments to suss the potential problem, by which time the sound of breaking glass was filling the air as the police broke into the front shop and began ushering the hostages out.

'Fuckin' cunt. Fuckin' cunt.'

Jyzer kicked viciously at Parlabane until eventually he rolled clear, then threw the door open to see his prisoners fleeing and the armed cops kneeling down to take aim. He slammed it shut again and pushed a table up against it, then backed into the room, indicating to Parlabane to crawl over against the wall to his right. Jyzer knelt down a few feet away, the gun pointing half-way between his prisoner and the door, his eyes shuttling between both targets.

'We've still got a hostage in here,' he shouted. 'Any o' yous cunts tries this door and we'll do 'im, right? We still want that fuckin' helicopter.'

'OK, OK, everybody stay calm,' appealed a voice from the other side of the door. 'Everybody just calm down. I'm pulling my marksmen back to outside the shop, so don't panic and do something we'll all regret.'

'I wouldnae regret shootin' you, ya cunt,' Jyzer hissed at Parlabane, who just smiled.

'Sorry, Jyzer, but in case you've no' worked it out, the *last* thing you can do is shoot me—I'm your only hostage. Soon as I'm out of the equation, it's you versus the bullets. That's unless you professionals can take out a team of trained marksmen with your stove-pipes there.'

Frustration was writ large in Jyzer's eyes. He clearly wished he could blow Parlabane away or, at the very least, finally silence him with a telling oneliner. He settled for:

'Fuckin' shut it.'

Then he called out to the cops. 'We're aw calm in here. Yous keep calm an' aw. An' get on wi' gettin' that helicopter.'

Tommy was hectically hunting through drawers and cupboards, having tried the handle on the only other door in the room.

'I cannae find the keys, Jyzer,' he gasped in a loud whisper.

'Well, they've got tae be here somewhere. Keep lookin'.'

'Couldn't possibly be on the person of one of your erstwhile hostages?' Parlabane suggested.

'Aw fuck,' Tommy sighed.

'Keep at it, Tommy, there'll be another set somewhere. Dinnae listen tae that cunt.'

'What were you wanting from the stationery cupboard, anyway?'

Parlabane asked. 'Checking there's no, eh, insurance bonds mixed in wi' the dug-licence application forms?'

'Would ye fuckin' shut it about the bonds? They were meant tae be here. Scottish Widows changed the delivery. They're worth thousands. Nae ID needed. Good as money.'

'That's right, they're transgotiable,' Tommy contributed.

'Shut it, Tommy, that's no the word. Keep lookin'. An' as for you, bigmooth, that's no' any stationery cupboard. Behind that door's the thing that's gaunny make you eat every wan o' your smart-cunt words.'

'What, proof that Madonna's got talent?'

'Naw. That door leads tae the underground railway. Belongs tae the Post Office, for sendin' stuff back and forward. Runs fae here doon tae the main sortin' depot at Brunswick Road, which is where we've got a motor waitin'. They'll still be coverin' the exits up here while we're poppin' up haufway doon Leith Walk. And wance we're there, you'll have outlived your usefulness, "lived" bein' the main word. Aye, ye're no so smart, noo, are ye?'

Parlabane shook his head, squatting on the floor against the wall.

'Underground railway?' he asked, grinning.

'Aye.'

'I've got two words for you, Jyzer: insurance bonds.'

'An' I've got two words for you: fuckin' shut it. Tommy, have ye fun' thae keys yet?'

'Sorry, Jyzer. I don't think there's a spare set.'

'Fuck it,' Jyzer said, getting to his feet. 'You watch him, Tommy.' Jyzer walked over to the locked door and pointed his shotgun at the metal handle.

'No, don't do that!' Parlabane shouted, too late.

Jyzer pulled his trigger and blasted the handle, then reeled away from the still-locked door, bent double and groaning.

'AAAAYAAA FUCKIN' BASTARD!' he screamed, falling to the floor, blood appearing from the dozens of tiny wounds where the pellets had ricocheted off the solid metal and back into his thighs, hands, wrists, abdomen and groin.

'STAY OOT!' Tommy shouted to the cops behind the door. 'STAY OOT. The hostage is awright. Just a wee accident in here. Just everybody keep steady, right?'

'Let's hear the hostage,' called the cop. 'Let's hear his voice.'

Tommy, looking increasingly like the least steady person on earth, waved the gun at Parlabane and nodded, prompting him to reply.

'I'm here,' Parlabane shouted.

'You OK, sir?'

'Do you really want me to answer that?'

'I mean, are you hurt?'

'No. But Jyzer here just learned a valuable lesson about the magic of the movies.'

'What?'

'That's enough,' Tommy interrupted, scuttling over to check on his writhing companion. 'What's the score wi' that helicopter?' he called.

'I think an air ambulance might be more appropriate,' Parlabane said.

'Fuckin' shut it,' Tommy hissed. It was the only part of Jyzer's role he had been so far able to assimilate.

'It's over, Tommy,' Parlabane said quietly. 'Your pal's in a bad way, there's polis everywhere, and I'm afraid you're 300 miles from the nearest underground postal railway, which is in London.'

'It's no'. There's wan here. We've had information.'

'Is everybody OK in there?' asked the policeman.

'STAY OOT!' Tommy warned again, his voice starting to tremble. 'The situation's no' changed. Stay oot.'

Jyzer continued to moan in the corner, convulsed also by the occasional cough.

'There's no such things as insurance bonds, Tommy,' Parlabane told him.

'Shut it. There is.'

'Where did you get this "information"?'

'That's ma business.'

'Did you pay for it? Is someone on a percentage?'

'Naw. Aye. The second wan.'

'Never done anything like this before, have you?'

Jyzer moaned again, eyes closed against the pain.

Tommy shook his head. He was starting to look scared, like he needed his Mammy to take him home.

'Somebody put you up to it? Somebody force you?'

'Naw,' he said defensively. 'We were offered this. Hand-picked. He gied us the information, an' we'd tae gie him forty per cent o' the cally efterwards.'

'You been inside before? Recently?'

'Aye. Oot six weeks. Baith ay us.'

'And I take it you weren't inside for armed robbery.'

He shook his head again.

Parlabane nodded. He reached into his pocket and pulled out his compact little mobile phone.

'Whit ye daein'? Put that doon.'

'Just let me call the cops outside, okay? Save us shoutin' through the wall the whole time.'

'Aye, awright.'

He dialled the number for Gayfield Square, explained the situation and asked to be patched through to the main man on-site.

'Are you sure you're all right, sir?' the cop in charge asked. 'What's your name? Do you need us to get a message to someone?'

'I'm fine. My name's Jack Parlabane. Yes, *that* Jack Parlabane, and spare me the might-have-knowns. I didn't *try* to get myself into this, it just happened. Now, Tommy here's not quite ready to end this, I don't think. But I was wondering whether you might want to scale down the ARU involvement out there. I've got a feeling you'll be needing them elsewhere fairly imminently.'

'Too late,' the cop informed him. 'Somebody hit the Royal Bank at the west end of George Street about fifteen minutes ago while we were scratching our arses back here. By the time any of our lot got there it was all in the past tense. We've been had.'

'You're not the only ones.'

'What was that?' Tommy asked.

'Bank robbery, Tommy,' he told him. 'A proper one. Carried out less than a mile from here while the police Armed Response Unit were holding their dicks outside a Post Office. Now who do you think could have been behind that? Same guy gave you "the information", maybe?'

'But . . . but . . . we . . .'

'You were right about being hand-picked, Tommy. And you can both take some satisfaction from the fact that you carried out the plan exactly as intended. Unfortunately, you were intended to fuck up. What were the instructions? Grab the mysterious insurance bonds, create a hostage

situation, keep the polis occupied, then escape via the magical underground railway? And were you given a specific date and time, perhaps?'

There was confusion in Tommy's eyes, but on the whole resignation was
starting to replace defiance. Jyzer gave a last mournful splutter and passed
out.

'Don't suppose you want to score a few points with the boys in blue by
telling them who set you up so they can get on to his tail?'

'Mair than ma life's worth.'

'Fair enough. But it's still over, Tommy. Jyzer needs medical attention.
The wounds might be superficial, but then again they might not. Come on.
Put the gun down.'

Tommy looked across at the unconscious Jyzer surrounded by blood-
stains on the beige carpet, then at the locked door, then back at his hostage.

'Ach, fuck it,' he rasped angrily, knuckles whitening as he gripped the
gun tighter.

Parlabane took an involuntary breath, his eyes locked on Tommy's.

'The cunt's name was McKay,' he said with a sigh. 'Erchie McKay. Met
him inside. He got oot last month, same as us.' Tommy put the shotgun
down on the floor and slid it across to Parlabane. 'Just make sure they
catch the bastart.'

At eight-thirty that evening, the nightly performance of 'Whoops
Checkov' was abandoned after a number of powerful stink-bombs were
thrown through the door of the auditorium by an unidentified male. It
was, the unidentified male admitted to the woman driving his getaway car,
childish and puerile, but then so is much of the Fringe.

Ron Butlin is the author of several novels, including The Sound of My Voice *and* Night Visits, *and some half-dozen collections of poetry and short stories. Besides his radio plays, much of his work has been broadcast in Britain and abroad (BBC World Service); his poetry and fiction have been translated into over ten languages. He has given readings in Europe, Canada and Australia and, through the auspices of the British Council, in Eastern Europe, France, Nigeria, Mauritius and Switzerland. This story comes from his collection,* Talk of the Devil.

How the Angels Fly In

By Ron Butlin

Neither of his guests wants to be here, that's obvious. Every time a cup or saucer clatters on to the hard shine of his formica table there's another awkward pause. But they are putting on a gallant show; compliments to his bachelor tidiness have been succeeded by Mark's hilarious account of his and the lovely Donna's rats-in-a-trap drive across town to get here this afternoon. Jordan catches the odd word; he is playing the host to perfection and appreciates their need for small-talk. He is not a cruel man.

It's been twenty-five years since he was at school with Mark, or rather with the boy Mark once was; he'd never met the lovely Donna before. They'd been going into Woolworth's when he caught sight of them; a

quick 'Long-time-no-see,' an invitation for them to drop round and the
follow-up phone call he'd made a few days later – and they hadn't a
chance. Too polite for their own good. But having agreed to come,
however reluctantly, they will be taking the opportunity to *view* him –
let's be clear about their motives even if they themselves aren't. Mark
continues gabbling on about the new one-way system, the new parking
problems. Sometimes Jordan turns the sound down, as it were, and just
watches. With no words to distract him, his guests' nervous mannerisms
and gestures are a give-away. Mark, for example, keeps turning ever so
slightly towards the door that leads to the hall and upstairs – not too
difficult to work out what's going on in *his* mind. As for the lovely Donna,
with her thick black hair and nice breasts already saying more than
enough, she needn't speak if she doesn't want to. She looks uncomfortable,
though, and avoids meeting his eye.

'Another piece of shortbread, Donna?' He smiles and pushes the plate in
her direction. Being a well brought-up little Miss she will accept the
kindliness of his manner and might even be feeling sorry for him. At
school Mark had the right haircut, the right jeans, the right trainers; he
went around with other boys like himself, the ones who played football
and had girlfriends. Jordan rarely addressed any of 'the boys' in case they
snubbed him; he hated them, and would have given anything to have been
one of them. Since returning to the town a year ago he has run into a fair
number of those 'boys', usually on a Saturday, in their casual weekend
sweatshirts and with wife and kids in tow. A few minutes' chat and they
can't wait to get away. No one was ever going to call round to say 'hello',
that's for sure. Mark's monologue is getting quite frantic, as if to ward off
the silence that is now part of the house itself. In normal circumstances the
rigours of traffic systems, off-zone parking and the like provide the
familiar shallows where the grown-up 'boys' of this world paddle around
for all they're worth, splashing loudly to make a reassuring noise for
themselves. But the circumstances that have brought them here today are
not normal, and so: gabble, gabble, gabble while looking far across the
green formica to the deeper waters where he, Jordan, calmly gazes back at
them in his unrivalled experience of life and, more importantly, of death.

'More tea?' He makes sure he's already started pouring before the lovely
Donna has a chance to refuse. 'So, Donna, how do you like living in our
town? How long have you been here now?'

She likes it. It's a nice town. She's been here fourteen years.

'So long? Almost a native, eh! The new Riverview Estate, I think you said. Beautiful houses in a beautiful setting – the old army barracks stood there when Mark and I were at school. Waste of a prime building site, it was. You'll be well settled in now, I expect?'

Yes, the neighbours are friendly but not too much, if he knows what she means. He nods and smiles. Near enough the town centre but still quiet and by itself. Another interested nod.

And so on. And so on. And so on.

When he feels ready he will start them on to the next stage of their visit, a tour of the house: both floors, ending up in the room directly above where they are now. Meanwhile he'd sit listening to their aimless chit-chat and his own equally aimless responses. Best of all would be to raise his hand for silence, and to hold everything just *there*: the conversation stopped in mid-sentence. A snap of the fingers and, transported as if by magic, the three of them would be upstairs, staring into that part of hell he had the courage to enter twenty-five years ago and has been trapped in ever since.

Instead, he has to let the chit-chat go on while the clock chimes another quarter of an hour done away with. He sits and they sit.

The tea and shortbread finished, it is time to turn off the gabble at source with a casual 'Would you like to see round the place?' Then, before they can make some excuse about leaving or putting him to unnecessary trouble, he stands up and motions Mark and the lovely Donna to rise from their places at the formica. 'The house was built at the end of last century; my parents added the extension.' With this casual mentioning of his parents – intended as a token of reassurance – the tour has begun.

He has ushered them into the dining-room to inspect the marble fireplace, the splendid shutters, the bow-windows and finally – star attraction! – the vast mahogany sideboard. What craftsmanship! He points out the delicacy with which every rose-petal and spray has been painstakingly carved, the intricate harmony of the different grains, the integrity of the entire piece as having been constructed without nail or glue. Naturally, he makes no comment on the cabinets smelling of mould, nor does he draw attention to the empty drawers whose velvet casings must have been stripped of the family cutlery not long after the evening he entered his parents' bedroom.

There are none of the customary framed photographs – if that's why the lovely Donna is glancing around the room. Weddings, christenings, anniversaries – his family has nothing to prove any more. Or hasn't that been explained to her yet? Poor Donna, wherever she looks she will be disappointed; polished surfaces reflect back a china shepherdess, a candlestick in its brass holder, dustbowls of pottery. The small-talk's been hastily resumed in response to the hollow echoing of their footsteps on the room's uncarpeted floor. Feeling mischievous, he interrupts with a question.

'And do you have any children?'

At once the lovely Donna stiffens, then almost immediately relaxes again. So, she does know. Mark must have told her after their unexpected meeting last week. Or did the coward wait until they were driving up and down the one-way streets this morning? 'By the way, dear, there's something about Jordan I should tell you . . .

His question, with its darker implications, was perfectly timed and has caught them unawares. There is a somewhat abrupt 'Not yet' from Mark, which is tempered by detail upon detail of a lifeplan calculated, so it seems, to take him and the lovely Donna well into the next century. A lifeplan – these paddlers in the shallows! They're out of their depth now all right! Glancing at each other in a way he's not supposed to know anything about, the pair of them! For *they* are a couple, *they* are special and have drawn a circle – completely invisible to the likes of him, of course – around themselves to keep themselves beyond harm. As if team-spirit, haircuts, designer labels, parking restrictions, marriage and the rest of it were enough to guide them and keep them safe! Such good, good people. Having brought them here, he will show them what really lies inside their careful little circles.

He was thirteen when he made his way along the upstairs corridor, eyes half-closed to conceal from himself the sharpness of the carving knife he held in his hand. There was no sound from his parent's bedroom; the madness that filled the house day after day with its screams, its rage and despair must have been pausing for breath. He reached for the door-handle. Until then he had tried his best to fit in: to read the signs and anticipate repentence, terror or whatever was required; to give a whispered 'Yes' in answer to every crazy accusation while silencing within himself the 'No' screaming to be heard. Had their madness at last become his own?

Was that what had made him slide open the sideboard drawer, lift out the carving knife from its velvet setting and come upstairs? He'd been nothing more than a child when, with tears running down his face, he hacked his way to the heart of the only circle he had known.

And so, twenty-five years later: left hand on the banisters, best foot forward and up he goes leading the way. Faded yellow wallpaper, repatterned by colourful streaks of damp, to his right; and to his left the solidity of varnished oak. He urges his guests forward, his voice talking about underfelt, carpets, rewiring and their voices dutifully fill in the gaps he leaves for them.

'I'm thinking of having the doors stripped back to the natural wood.'

'We did that ourselves a couple of years ago. Lots of work but worth it, wasn't it, Danna?'

'Yes. Looks nice when it's finished.'

And so the landing is reached.

Then the first room. His voice jostling theirs into response to make sure every second's accounted for. Their unspoken question: 'Was it here?'

Along the corridor.

The next room is reached.

Then another few yards.

The last room. His voice continues firm, steady, obliging; he explains that he is preparing things for the decorators. He points out the unpainted walls, the blocked-up fireplace and the emptiness where his parents' furniture had stood: the chairs, dressing table, wardrobe, their bed. That much he tells them in a voice that doesn't falter.

He pauses, and can hardly believe it when what he has most hoped for at this point actually occurs: a sudden and visible arrest of feeling on the faces of these, his first guests. They are deeply moved. For several seconds no one speaks. He waits. They know what happened here. Surely they can sense what showing them this room must mean to him?

The lovely Donna has taken a few hesitant steps forward. She's pointing to the skylight set into the sloping roof; it's rusted solid and stuck slightly open. She's said something.

'Pardon?'

'That's how the angels fly in,' she repeats. 'When I was little that's what my grandad used to say when someone had left a window open.' She's looking at him and smiling.

'Angels?' What's the woman talking about? What's she doing here if that's all she has to say? 'Angels?'

He should calm himself or in a minute he'll be stammering.

'Yes, they were invisible, of course, but grandad said if we listened hard enough we would hear their wings as they flew around us.'

He can feel sweat standing out on his brow, clamminess on his hands; and he's trembling now.

Mark grins: 'That would be something, eh!'

Can't they see what's happening to him? He tenses himself but the shaking's started going through his whole body. Can't they see it? Can't they do something?

No. They're gabbling and grinning and giving advice on redecoration.

A slight draught's coming into the room, bringing with it the scent of cherry blossom from the back garden – a sickly, choking stench. If the skylight wasn't so high he'd make the pair of them watch him jam it shut. Then he'd frogmarch them out of the room, along the corridor, down the stairs and away to wherever the hell they came from. He needs stepladders, tools; he'll wrench the window back into place, nail it shut, board it up if he has to. No more angels, no more guests.

He holds the door open for them to leave. He must hurry. Quickly, before the cherry blossom gets stronger and fills the whole house so he cannot breathe. Quickly, before the angels come, the lightest touch of whose wings brings the threat of forgiveness.

Linda Cracknell lives in Aberfeldy, Perthshire, where she works as Education Officer for an environmental charity. Born in the Netherlands, she came to live in Scotland in 1991 via Surrey, Devon and Tanzania. Her first story to be published, Life Drawing, *won the Macallan/Scotland on Sunday* Short Story Competition *in 1998.*

Death Wish

By Linda Cracknell

Will it be your body or the rucksack they find first? The rucksack, unfastened and abandoned. Left on a rocky outcrop not far off the path, next to a half-drunk bottle of Vittel water and a small pile of orange peel. Without that clue it could take ages before you're discovered in the thick forest below. It must be a fall of 500 metres. Straight down the sun-kissed cliff. Perhaps it'll be a walker who comes across you. With tanned legs and dusty boots, he'll be reclaiming the path from melt-water landslides in the Spring sunshine. He'll recoil from the lacerated limbs, still hanging heavy in the low branches. The discovery might take long enough that it's the smell that makes him notice. He'll run for help, making uneven progress as the retches fold him double.

There's a third possibility, beyond the discovery of the body or the rucksack. The hotel staff will notice the bed unslept in. The first night they'll shrug away a holiday romance, but after the second they'll call in the police. They need to be paid if the room's not occupied.

But it's most likely to be the rucksack that leads to the body. A group of scouts from Switzerland sent off for the day to practice their map-reading skills will see it when they pass in the morning. They won't think much of a small rucksack left near the path. But when they retrace their steps later and it's still there, they'll cluster around its open top, not touching, but peering in as if the contents will reveal what they should do. They'll debate it for a while, until one of them is bold enough to pick it up, clip up the straps, and carry it down to the town. It will end up with the police and trigger a search party to swarm through the forest below.

For the detective it'll be a 'lucky-bag' of sorts. He'll fix his eyes on the wall in front, as his fingers close blind on each item, unpacking them on to the formica table. When he's sure it's empty, he'll put the rucksack on one side and frown at the collection on the table.

- Sun cream; factor 8. (When they find the body, perhaps they'll notice the two red patches on the upper arms where the rucksack worked with sweat to rub off the cream and allow the sun to bite.)
- A French–English dictionary. The Larousse mini series; practical and lightweight.
- A jumper. Orange and woollen. Hand-framed in Scotland.
- Sunglasses. (But you'll still be wearing them perhaps? Posing in Raybans even to the death.)
- A small sponge bag. Lipstick and tampons inside. Female, then (my dear Watson).
- A map of Lac d'Annecy.
- A wallet. (The detective will feel more confident of an ID now.) French francs inside but no cards, no papers. Left behind in the security of a hotel room.
- Two postcards. Unwritten. One is an aerial shot of the lake enclosed by its amphitheatre of peaks. Colour a bit brash. The other shows the pretty canal-side and its terrace bars in the old town of Annecy. (The coroner, brought over from Britain to conduct the investigation, will resist a moment's guilt as he or she

takes a beer there in the evening, enjoying the sunshine and the drift past of smiling tourists. You have to take a break from death.)

- A plastic carrier bag with the remains of a baguette, a piece of cheese (Emmental) and a Swiss army knife.
- A black and red hard-backed notebook. Ruled.

The notebook. Without it they'll know nothing. All they'll know is that you're British (or at least English-speaking), female, apparently on holiday. And then the notebook will take away all the mystery. They'll get to know you with unearned ease. It might not provide your name, address, next of kin, but it will identify you. They'll know where you've been. They might even mark your route with those fat pins with coloured heads on a map on the enquiry room wall. And they'll stand and gaze at the pattern. 'No ordinary holiday, that. As if she was running from something,' they'll say.

They'll know what you've been doing – the days sitting alone at café tables, dragging your rucksack in and out of trains and buses. Hanging your washed-through underwear overnight on a piece of string tied between radiator and wash stand in the hotel room. They'll know how you felt when you looked at your cold sores in the mirror, and pulled the two grey hairs from your fringe. They'll know about your tussle with sleep and the encounters with long-forgotten people in your dreams.

And they'll know what it is you've done; what it was that dispatched you for a 'short break' to France. They'll know how you killed in cold blood. The way you just wanted it dead. And the people who shadow you since, waiting to punish, pushing you to the edge. And how you knew they were there, even though they hid, appearing only as a penumbra, a shady outline, behind bus drivers, waiters, fellow tourists.

When they find the body, they'll identify you with the help of your chipped front tooth. Your mother will choke into her hanky on the phone to the British Embassy. She'll remember not only the *fact* of the tooth, but *how* you chipped it. Running up the garden path in answer to her call, to see the kittens being born. You tripped and crashed on to the front step. But she cradled you in anyway, dripping tears and blood, to witness the mysterious moment. The high mews of new life in a cardboard box stilled your sobs. And afterwards she took you to an emergency dentist.

The air is sun-dried, the cool Spring wind suspended by the rocks. Two butterflies chase each other, prettifying the vertical panorama. Sky, to Haute-Savoie peaks, to lake. You're small and still amongst the birds who tumble and glide in the thermals thrown up by the edge in front of you, the gap from cliff top to lake floor. They have the nonchalance of Dead Sea swimmers. Cars buzz along the hazy lakeside below, inhabiting a world of different perspectives: roadside restaurants, boat hire and views only upwards.

You came from that world this morning, before you reached stillness here. Ducks cowered from the heat, their heads and necks swallowed by the lake. The grass in the low-lying meadows was starred with Spring flowers like the Swiss chocolate boxes brought as presents from European airports in your childhood. The meadow beckoned you to tumble and roll in its length and moisture, to press your nose to the wild garlic. It tried to trick you, like the men in the town, with the fresh smell they left in the air as they passed you, their tanned faces crying out to be kissed. A pretence that it was safe to linger. But you resisted. Your feet continued upwards on the rocky path, the sweat drying on your face. Until you found this place amongst rocks and dry grass on the summit of the cliff. This is the place.

You peel an orange as you wait. The citrus oil bursts into your face, but these days, since the death, it no longer makes you feel sick. Your body is your own again. You can hear the dryness around you. The air crackles with it. The crispness of brush and branch betrays movement. You know that before long it'll be human movement. A noise halts your breathing, the lack of human voice as tangible as a shouted warning. But when you look over your shoulder, there's no one. A bird or lizard making small tracks through the grass. You breathe again, but the waiting hurts.

You wonder what will happen before the spread-eagle in blue air. It'll be a challenge for the coroner. Injuries consistent with a fall of so many metres. But did you step? Or slip? Or were you pushed?

The sun drowses your eyelids and your body succumbs to something like sleep. Your senses startle you awake when an ant's jaw closes on your bare calf or the dry panic of the undergrowth sits you upright, swivels your head. And the images are there again, breezing over you with the rise and fall of consciousness. You see your mother's back in the familiar herring-bone overcoat. As she turns, she shows you a slight frown in a blank face, and then she walks on, away from you up the home street, her carrier-bag concealing comforts from the corner shop.

Through the eyelashes, a flutter of blue sky, a crackle near your ear and then you're looking up from a white bed, at a nurse, and she smiles and sinks a needle into your arm, casting you several leagues deep into feather pillows. And you wake up in another room, surrounded by women's bodies inert on trolleys, and a thick pad between your legs, stuck to you with what must be blood. And something is nudging to the front of your mind. A circumstance. A curled-up body, shrimp-like, in a metal pan somewhere. You don't see it but you know you're responsible for it. You wanted to kill it. Wished it dead.

Then your eyes are blue-wide and they fix on the arc of a paraglider canopy, luminous green above you. It pirouettes, the human centre dark against the sun-green. Very dark. The pilot swings outwards to side-fill the canopy. He mocks you with his slowness, knowing that he must finally come down. He sweeps and circles, plays with the thermals, accelerating the threat high above you. His crossed legs beneath the harness become indiscernible. You know that he smiles, his head bent forward to observe his prey. And you're lizard-long in the sun near the cliff edge, face upwards. You lie and wait as he spirals up and up.

And there's a sense of relief; an end in sight. Ever since the clinic, you've been in a series of endless waiting rooms, one adjoining the next. Waiting for the moment.

And when some hours have passed, the low sun has changed the colours on the lake and ruffled the oak woodland, mellowed the cliff colour. You see yourself as the shadowy paraglider must, standing on the extreme edge, facing outwards. And you're holding something high in both hands. Small petals break away from it, float outwards from your hands, bright against the shadows, dark against the lake glare. They dance in the light and the upward currents before taking a chaotic journey outwards and downwards towards the lake. As you tear and release the last pieces of notebook, you stand erect on the cliff top, arms stretched upwards, your stillness caught in the turn and curl of a galaxy of paper stars. You're ready now. And a small distance behind you, a rucksack lies open, waiting to be discovered.

Chris Dolan's short story collection, Poor Angels, *was published by Polygon in 1995, the year in which he also won the Macallan/*Scotland on Sunday *Award. He adapted his story* Sabina *for the stage, winning a Fringe First in 1996, and the play has since been performed in Spain and Italy. His first novel,* Ascension Day, *was published in August 1999 (Hodder Headline Review). He lives in Glasgow.*

Conviction

By Chris Dolan

I open the door briskly these days. It's an old one I picked up and restored, an art-nouveau glass panel in it. You could, if you wanted, peer through the fleur-de-lis stained design to see who's just rung your bell. A thing I never do. The person outside clocks you checking them out and that's the last impression I want to give. Still, in the split second before opening up, I knew it was the police. Height, bulk, hats and all in black.

No overdoing it now. Nod, open the door wide, step back to let the good constable and lady constable in. They bow their heads ever so subtly – while they're crossing the thresh. Minute they're inside, though, the change is dramatic. The smiles drop and the humble stooping straightens sharply. They case the joint, check out my decor, ornaments, pictures. Looking for clues. Suddenly, I'm the guilty one again.

I almost feel like telling them, as I lead them towards the sitting room, well of course I am. But it's all right, officers, everything's in hand. It'll all be sorted.

My hall's wee, hankie-sized, a space to separate the doors of the sitting room, kitchen, bedroom, loo and the only cupboard of any size in the whole flat. Elbowing each other to take hats off and undo buttons I can sense them holding the smallness of the place against me. A flat so obviously, so permanently, for one. All that brazen sponged orange on the walls, colour-washed floor-boards. Person like me – I should have seen what was coming. Could have averted the whole thing.

In the living room, the woman smiles at me, full-on attention, eye-to-eye while the geezer looks down behind chairs, scans the mantelpiece.

'Want a cuppa?' I say, and cuppa sounds very dodgy.

They ask for coffee and I go to the kitchen. I can hear them moving about the minute I'm gone, hear them mumbling. I'm pouring milk into the jug on the tray when they start laughing. It makes me stop, take stock. The tray's too fussy. I put the cups and saucers back, take out mugs instead. I didn't ask if they take milk or not, but no matter. All PCs take milk and two sugars, WPCs just milk. Then I decide to leave the third mug out. I don't like instant and I'm worried about drinking in front of them, what it'll reveal. I bet, these days, all constables get a crash course in Freud.

At the door, I inspect the kitchen for evidence. Shopping I've still to put away – medical stuff from Boots, first aid etcetera, new plastic chopping board and knife, scissors, loo rolls, shoe polish. Nothing that'd seem out of the ordinary. Taking the mugs through to the room my eye catches a brochure lying by the phone on the hall table. Glasgow University Department of Adult and Continuing Education. My name and address in big letters and a stamp in bright red, 'Contains Course Materials'. Shouldn't have left that lying around. I've read somewhere that criminals are self-improvers. It's common knowledge. Criminals, outcasts, those kind of people, never happy with their lot. They're disaffected, can't work the system, try too hard. I knock the envelope down the back of the table with my elbow. Walk into the room trying to look like an insider, someone not bearing a grudge. Or maybe that's wrong. Maybe that's why they keep coming back. It isn't natural, after what happened, not to bear a grudge.

'Nice flat, Mr Mathieson,' says the WPC to me. And the PC says to her, 'Andrew.'

He's met me before, she hasn't. He was there on the night and, later, at the hospital. He's pulling rank and experience and at the same time sucking up to me, palsy-walsy. Do I know his first name, too? He probably told me. Can't remember. And was there an inflection in that 'nice' of hers? Flat too tidy, not manly enough for her? Are criminals known for having considered decor? It'd make sense – dissimulation, premeditation. All that.

The WPC takes her coffee and goes to the window.

'Some view,' her companion says, from his seat. Denis. That's it. Don't think he's been up here, at the flat, before. I remember at the hospital he couldn't look me in the eye. Still can't. 'Nice view of the park.'

They're talking over my head for my benefit. It's a routine. Any minute, one of them, probably him, will turn round and ask me the one devastatingly insightful cop-show question that'll have me collapsing in a heap, confessing everything.

Nice view of the park. Is that what they're here for? Confirm the scene of the crime can be observed from the victim's window? Of course it fucking can. Should I tell them how I get up every night and stare out that very window, gawp, sickened, down into that park? Tell them I haven't slept for a month, every rustle of a leaf down there tearing though my head, every slug eating at me.

'What can I do for you, officers?' I say, sitting. They're right, of course. I've lived here overlooking that park for years. How could I not have known?

'We've some information for you, Andrew.'

Then the WPC does a strange thing. She returns to her seat and, I swear blind, catches my eye as she crosses the room, puts her hand on her skirt as she sits and lets it ride too far up her thigh. It stays too far up for a moment, she glances again at me, then pulls it back down, looks over at her colleague. They were trying to judge my reaction. Did it turn me on? Was I straight? Was I pervy? Was I the kind of guy who'd hang around parks at night?

It's a no-win situation. Notice her stockings – dodgy; don't notice – pervy. I'm weighing up in my mind now whether or not to have done with it and treat them to an in-depth description of my sex-life. The reason I live alone. Admit a lifelong apprehension about the whole physical kerfuffle. Explain how it's easier just to say goodnight and come home to a nightcap and my own, safe, company. I'm seriously considering launching right into it when Dennis says, 'We've got one of them.' Jesus. Which one? As if it mattered. It didn't matter then, and it doesn't matter now. The black-haired one? The skull one? The one I see going to work every morning, standing calmly, civilly, at the bus-stop, not recognising me standing at the stop across the way, heading in the other direction.

'How do you know?'

The WPC leans forward.

'He's got a record, Mr Mathieson. He can't account for his whereabouts on the night, and he fits one of the descriptions you gave us.'

'It'd help, Andrew, if you'd press charges.'

We've been through all this. They say, Why come to us in the first place and I say I didn't, you found me. Lying in the park. I was reported. Don't want to be dragged through it all again, and anyway you won't be able to convict and I'll be in greater danger. They say if I don't behave like a responsible citizen other folk will be in danger. What I *don't* say is those kind of folk are in danger anyway, because they carry the danger around with them. There'll always be a brute loitering out there that'll get the scent of their weakness, act on it.

All I want to do now is make it known that I did nothing to bring this on. Nothing to invite the inevitable happening. Sure, it was stupid walking through the park, but it wasn't that late and it was only for a few yards. Been doing it for years. From the bridge – just there, under our noses – to the gate, across the street. No distance. I just want everyone to say, Sorry pal. The bastards were always going to get you. I don't want court cases and evidence and punishment and digging any deeper. I've already got the solution – I don't need any other.

'You're not dealing with your anger.'

The WPC, that. So they *do* do foundation psychoanalysis. Then she adds a quiet, 'Andrew.'

Can you image them, the constables, in their shabby lecture room and their woolly suits and brains, sergeant up at the board with a pointer, giving out on the difference between animus and anima, Oedipus, fixations? And all the while they're thinking: bottom line is, it's a bunch of psychos out there, anyone who doesn't live in a semi in Bishopbriggs, go to the footy and drink in the lounge bar on a Saturday night.

'In the long term, please believe me, it'll be much better for you if you purge yourself of the whole thing.'

I listen to this tosh, trying to smile at her, clenching the arms of my chair. Can't even look at *him*. Denis, watching his inferior officer giving me the old trauma-and-purge routine. Poor buggered sweetie-wifie prefers talking to a female.

'Do what you have to do and get back to your old life, Andrew.'

They can't understand it was my old life that brought this on. Every step I'd taken in my entire existence led up to that crucial night. My gait when I was learning to walk, my accent when I was beginning to talk, the first clothes I bought, friends I chose, the way I happened to look that day. The scarf and the hat. Hair too long. She asks me to go over again exactly what happened that night.

I could tell her to fuck off. I'd be perfectly within my rights. But I don't want to. I want to clobber her with the story, wipe that smarmy look off her face. So I lock her eyes to mine, and I tell her how it was just after the clocks went back in October and it was darker than I'd expected, but still only sixish, and I was on the shortcut path between the bridge and the gate across from my close, and I add in, 'Where you say the trees are so nice.'

Denis is locked in, too. Sitting quiet. I say there are these five guys coming towards me and the funny thing is I don't even suspect anything. They look like five ordinary blokes, in their twenties. I'm about to mumble 'Hi' to them, as you do. They part for me to pass and with hindsight now I can see that parting was too clear-cut, planned. I'm about to pass when one of them sticks their foot out, trips me up. I'm not even too freaked by that, just reckon they're a bunch of stroppy gits. They'll have a laugh and shout 'arse bandit' and be on their way. Live in this city and you have to put up with that kind of crap. You're even supposed to celebrate it. Crazy, spunky kids.

But I've got it all wrong. They start laying into me. Kicks and punches and spitting. They're not angry, not at first. They're kind of exhilarated. Like they've been planning this thing for ages and this is their big moment. I'm hanging on to that faint glimmer of hope – they don't sound that angry. Maybe they'll be sated quickly, move on.

Denis chips in, 'You said before you got the impression they knew you, these men?'

I meant, the impression I got was they were men on a mission. That maybe, yeah, they'd seen me before. Last officer I spoke to said that was common after an attack. Paranoia. Jesus, aren't we all just agony aunts this weather?

'Anyone you can think of who might hold a grudge against you, Andrew?'

I'm not going to mention the guy at the bus-stop. I couldn't prove anything, and anyway I'd never noticed him before the incident. Perhaps he's been across the way from me all these years, seething at my coats or shoes or how I comb my hair, my stance. I look at Denis, then at the WPC, try to pick up where I left off. I take a deep breath. I'm off kilter now, beginning to wonder if I shouldn't button my lip. I carry on, but with less conviction.

'The punches and kicks stopped for a moment, but they were still laughing, calling me names. I managed to look up.'

Then I turned and looked at the woman officer.

'What did you say your name was again?'

'WPC Girven. Anne Girven.'

'All five of them, Anne, were standing over me with their penises out. Hard-ons, all of them, coming at me.'

Give her her due, she didn't blink and I told her how they were all rubbing themselves, gearing themselves up, how they stopped laughing and clenched their faces, got enraged at the tricky business of getting the keks off me without having to delicately undo the buttons. Ordering me to do it, screaming at me. How they jostled amongst themselves, frightened, for pecking order. Tried laughing when they told me it wasn't because they fancied me, how I was tighter than their wives and, as they came down on me and they ran out of fucks and cunts and poofters all they were left with was the worst possible thing they could think to call me. Ya woman.

Then, of course, there was the tricky business of me coming. It's true. I ejaculated, and if I ejaculated then I must have been enjoying it, and if I was enjoying it then maybe it wasn't an attack at all but a group session in the park at dusk that just got a little out of hand. I turned to Denis, spoke to him. Thought, the hell with it, I'm about to clear this whole mess up tonight anyway so I might as well get everything off my chest. I told him directly, I was excited, Denis. I must've been. A little at least. Somewhere inside me. Somewhere between the terror and the praying because I thought they might kill me and God knows I'm still waiting for the HIV test, so maybe they have. I was crying and I was in pain and bleeding and petrified and felt as if they were an alien species, that I was the only human being left on the planet and come to think of it maybe I am. I was lonely and wet and ashamed and angry and they were tearing me up and filling me full of their muck and spitting on me, drooling and punching me when they came; peed on me before they left. But I came, didn't I? That was obvious when they found me lying there. I had climaxed.

'Charge them. Get them, Andrew.'

Poor officers. They had to do something. Desperate for action. A name in their notebooks – my name, my attacker's, anyone's, made no difference. A process to start. They didn't have an end in sight, like I did. I took the mugs back through to the kitchen, keeping a grip of myself. Denis follows me through, puts a hand on my shoulder. He's tenser than I am.

'You've got to have the strength of your convictions, Andrew.'

Conviction, that's what we all wanted. Everyone I've ever met in my whole life has been so cocksure of what needed to be done, how things were. I've never been. They want convictions, and that's not something I'm big on.

At the front door, more declarations of them being on my side, prepared to do whatever it takes to nail these guys. But I can tell they feel even more distant from me than when they arrived. Just before she steps over the thresh, Girven notices the envelope down the back of the hall table, picks it up, glances at it, hands it to me. I thank her, thank them both and close the door. I watch them thud away down the close, drenched in yellow through the fleur-de-lis.

The envelope makes me feel better. 'Introductory Course in Fine Art'. Looking forward to that. Starts in January. I'll be there all right. Wild horses couldn't keep me away. I'll be there, a new person, all this behind me.

I tidy up after the officers, plump up cushions, reset the curtains, go back into the kitchen and start the preparations. I get the books down from the shelf, look out some old brandy and a bottle of schnapps brought back from Germany yonks ago. I've only myself to blame. People don't like you to be uncertain, open to interpretation. They want you to be sure of yourself, take sides, be in camps. I sometimes annoy people. I've always known that. Folk just want to teach me a lesson. Buck up my ideas.

I've got my little coterie, Roz and Phyllis and Paul. They like me well enough. I can be a laugh, when the mood takes. I get the phone and check that Roz's number still rings out when I press number 1. She'll be home soon. Poor girl, this might be the night she'll miss 'Corry'. It's the third time I've done this, got everything ready, and it's possible I'll cop out again. I get a basin from the bathroom, take out the disinfectants and bandages from the Boots bags, open the first aid book at the right page, get wet and dry towels ready. Make sure my jacket's got my house keys and wallet in it, the name of my doctor, yellow pages open at 'Emergency Services'. Then I start sipping the schnapps. Apricot. Sweet. Warms me through. Feeling determined now. Swallow a couple of Nurofens, boil up a saucepan of water and Dettol, put my new expensive knife and scissors in the pot. Loosen my trousers. Nearly ready now, stand there swaying, drinking, hugging myself, unzip my flies, scared.

Janice Galloway was born in Ayrshire and is resident in Glasgow. Her first novel, The Trick is to Keep Breathing, *was published in 1990 by Polygon and won the MIND/ Allen Lane Book of the Year award, as well as being shortlisted for the Whitbread First Novel prize. Her second novel,* Foreign Parts, *won the 1994 McVitie Prize, and in the same year she won the E.M. Forster Award.*

Someone Had To

By Janice Galloway

Blue eyes.

Right from the start her mother said, from the word go that was what people noticed. Took after her dad, she said: those big blue eyes, that LOOK on her. Not blinking. Fixed.

People sentimentalise; children and animals it's what they do. She may not speak much but she knows EVERY WORD YOU SAY. Her mother said that. Kind of thing you say about spaniels. Biddable things. Pets. They sentimentalise. It's easier than looking, REALLY LOOKING, seeing what there is to see. Little pinpoints, little drill holes. Sucking

you in. Knowing what they're doing. Knowing EVERY WORD YOU
SAY.

I tried. I gave her a fair chance. Took her out with the rest of us, the whole
family so to speak, she had outings, money spent. Not that she appreciated
it but she got it all the same. She never relaxed somehow. Difficult,
withdrawn. Never said THANK YOU FOR TAKING ME WITH YOU
UNCLE FRANK. Never said anything much at all. Never see that in the
papers. Clumsy, awkward, a social EMBARRASSMENT. Shyness they
called it. They said she was SHY. I lived with it remember, I was there.
Nobody else bothered then, nobody else even LOOKED but I DID. If
they'd looked they'd have seen but they chose not to. Left it to me. I was
the only one who saw what was coming. And I saw all right. I saw it every
DAY.

I'm not an unreasonable man.
    I argued.
    I said to her mother YOU need to do something about it she's YOUR
kid SHE NEEDS SEEING TO before things get out of hand. I told her it
wouldn't do. LET HER KEEP GOING THE WAY SHE'S HEADED I said
and we'll ALL BE SORRY. That STARING all the time like I'd done
something wrong. Those silences. They're unnatural in a girl her age, I
said, and that WATCHING ME. WATCHING. Like I'd no right to say
what was what in my OWN HOME. I said Linda that's how it STARTS
how ROT SETS IN. It needs pinching out at source. DUMB INSOLENCE
is the WORST KIND, the WORST I said and you're her mother. You just
let her DO IT. She has a NEED TO DEFY I said, a need to set you against
me, Linda, out of JEALOUSY I said. SPITE. You have to harden your heart
for your own good. For HER good. I ONLY HIT HER WHEN SHE'S
NAUGHTY I said, it's not SOMETHING I ENJOY. Look I said LOOK at
least with me she KNOWS WHAT WILL HAPPEN. If she keeps STARING
like that she KNOWS what the CONSEQUENCES WILL BE. She's the
oldest I said she ought to be an EXAMPLE. You can't keep on threatening
her with something she's not scared of. All right I said. Have it your own
way. If you can't I will I said she WON'T EAT with us any more. If she
won't learn one way, she'll learn another. She'll COME ROUND QUICK
ENOUGH when she's hungry. Go sparing rods and she'll SPOIL. You'll

destroy any chance we have of TEACHING HER ANY RESPECT. She'll thank us for it in the end. So I put her in the corner and she went. She knew I meant what I said all right and she went. But it didn't stop. You know what she did? Just stood there. Stood there stock still and WATCHED us eating, WATCHED US, you couldn't think straight, so you couldn't enjoy your food. None of us could. Why SHOULD I turn my back in my own home I said SHE can FACE THE WALL I said but it was just the same. Stubborn. HOURS she could spend, HOURS in the same place staring at the SAME PLACE so you knew she was doing it to get on your NERVES. Don't push me Kimberly, I said. I know what you're doing you don't fool ME. But she pushed. It was in her nature. A NEED TO DEFY. So I put her in the cupboard it was only for an hour or so and it was for ALL OF US I said I AM NOT LOCKING THE DOOR LINDA I said just putting the light off till she sees some SENSE you've got to be cruel to be kind I said but it was still no good. Quiet as a mouse for the first hour or so, the first couple of times then she starts again. She starts WHINING. WHINING. That's what she did. This noise in the cupboard like a collared bitch, getting louder and louder and plainly CALCULATED TO ANNOY. Even when you opened the door you warned her STOP THAT NOW KIMBERLY DO YOU HEAR ME she just kept WHINING pushing her back into the wall, knowing and INVITING IT JUST THE SAME keeping STARING to see if she was HAVING AN EFFECT. I said to her mother I said LINDA she KNOWS what she's doing. I wouldn't put up with that from YOU I said you go giving in to her now and godknows where it'll end. SOMEONE has to mean what they say I said and you starting up won't help all the time this whimpering going on in there, proving something, turning the screw. LINDA I SAID DON'T MAKE ME SHOUT I said. I don't want to have to force you. BUT SHE'LL STAY IN THERE TILL SHE'S SORRY. Somebody HAS TO BE consistent I said KIMBERLY THAT'S YOUR LAST WARNING and she knew I meant it. She knew all right. The whining stopped and I shut the door I said YOU'LL GET OUT WHEN YOU PROVE YOU CAN BE TRUSTED and I went to read my paper. You can't let these things get to you. But the next thing we were in bed when it started the next thing it beggars belief but it's true she started SCRATCHING I swear with her SCRATCHING DO YOU KNOW WHAT SHE DID? She CLAWED THE CUPBOARD DOOR with her NAILS SHE CLAWED THROUGH TO THE WOOD. Don't tell me that's NORMAL scraping her NAILS on the PAINT till they bled you can't tell me that is NORMAL FOR A SIX-YEAR-OLD CHILD. THEY KNOW THE DIF-FERENCE BETWEEN RIGHT AND WRONG. STOP THAT KIMBERLY I said that NOISE like RATS like it followed you to every room in the house I was calm I said STOP THAT KIMBERLY till it was more than FLESH AND BLOOD could stand. JESUSCHRIST LINDA I said it's not even as if she was MINE WHAT MORE AM I EXPECTED TO DO? You switch the TV louder and you still know what for, you still KNOW WHAT SHE'S DOING. So the last night it starts and I said DON'T PUSH ME KIMBERLY down the hall I pressed my mouth to the door I whispered DON'T DO IT PLEASE. I said PLEASE. I begged. And she just KEPT GOING. And that was it.

I put my hand on the doorknob.
I turned the key.

She was sitting next to the hoover. STAND UP KIMBERLY but she didn't. And I hit her NOT hard not to begin with but she just LOOKS not even FLINCHING when you TOLD her what would happen so I did it again STAND UP KIMBERLY curling in a corner NOT EVEN TRYING TO STAND UP just watching while I shook her, I lifted her up put the cigarette on to the skin of the wrist it was MEANT TO BE A LESSON all she needed to do was say she was sorry to STOP not knowing when to STOP the nape of her neck blistering the INSIDE OF HER black mouth open not saying a word just WATCHING while I DON'T TELL ME IT'S NORMAL FOR A CHILD NOT TO CRY OUT.

I SAID TO YOUR MOTHER I SAID SHE'S LET YOU OFF WITH MURDER. THIS IS ALL YOUR FAULT I said and our eyes met.

So it was me.

I told her to run the bath but she wouldn't. So I did it.
I filled it with boiling water. I put on the kettle. Someone had to.
Someone had to do something.

I ran the bath. I lifted her up.

Those big blue eyes still staring up like butter

wouldn't

melt

Iain Grant is a writer and musician who lives in Edinburgh. He has also worked as a journalist and a boiler cleaner. His first novel, Small Town Antichrist *(Oil Publishing), was published in 1999.*

I Shall Fear No Evil

By Iain Grant

There were three of them, a smaller audience than he preferred. On the other hand, they were chained to their chairs, so there would be nothing to distract them from his jokes. Apart, of course, from the fact that Big Malky was lurking behind him, but then Big Malky was also an essential part of the evening's entertainment. Not that Big Malky was famed for his sense of humour. Indeed, Big Malky rarely even smiled. Tad, though, was determined to have a good time, come what may. 'Ah like mah work,' he'd just told them, 'an Ah like tae throw maschel intae it. No' that a wee runt like maschel takesch a loat o throwin.'

Tad loved having an audience. Entertainment ran in his blood. Every inch of his four-foot-two-and-a-half frame was dedicated to his vocation in comedy. As soon as he'd come in this evening and been gloomily greeted by Big Malky, Tad had gone into his routine.

'Good evenin, ladiesch and genlemen,' he'd said, scanning the horizon. 'Hing oan a wee mo there, 'ersch nae ladiesch. N'ermind, eh? Ah'm schtill dead pleasched tae be here wi yousche all tonight, an Ah'm dead schure we're gauny hae wurschelsch a loat o laughsch. Ma namesch Valley, by the way, Tad Valley. They call me Valley o the Schadow o Death.'

He always paused here for dramatic effect, then said, 'No no no, jischt joakin ladsch, jischt joakin. Ah'm too wee tae cascht a schadow. Boom boom. Titter ye not, though, titter ye not. Schettle doon, schettle doon. Schee me? They call me Tad. Schort fer tadpole, ye know.'

True though this was, it got a laugh from one of the three lads in front of him. There may have been an element of relief in the reaction, but Tad was pleased to have got off to a good start. He liked these boys already.

Arranging what he liked to call his 'props' (to wit: his knife, his pliers, his ukelele and a bunch of bananas) on his table, he entertained the boys with his 'banana, ukelele; ukelele, banana' tribute to the late, great Tommy Cooper. He was hoping they'd still be able to walk by the time he and Big Malky had finished with them. They probably would, because Tad and Big Malky were masters of their profession. Big Malky knew just how far you could go without causing too much permanent damage, other than to the occasional kneecap or testicle. The two of them worked very well together. If there was a problem at all, it was that Big Malky felt Tad was spending too much time on the wisecracks and not leaving enough for the torturing. Big Malky had had words with him about it only the other day.

But then, in a way, it was Big Malky's fault that Tad – who had always had a gift for making people laugh – was here making the wisecracks at all. One of the first things Big Malky had said to him was there were two keys to success in the torturing game, and one of them was to get yourself a trademark. People notice you better that way, they listen to what you're saying. You're after results, after all. Tad saw the sense of it, and had seen straight away that the thing to do was to utilise his gift for clowning. It worked, too. He was very funny. His impression of George Formby was almost uncanny. People notice that kind of thing.

Of course, they also noticed the fact that he was a dwarf.

Tad practised his act in front of a full-length mirror. He made no secret of the fact. He used it as part of his patter. 'Obviously,' he would say, 'it schno a big full-length mirror, itsch a wee full-length mirror. Even then, Ah huv tae schtand oan a boax tae schee maschel. Schtill, Ah think it worksch OK.' Then – a tribute to another of his idols, this – he'd ask his audience, 'Whit dae ye think of it so far?' If they said 'ruggish', the correct answer, he'd remember to treat them special later on.

His delivery was . . . distinctive – his lisp and ill-fitting dentures gave him a unique way with a joke. Now that he was making money, of course, he could afford proper dentures, but he made sure he always wore the ill-fitting ones when he went to work. When his victims had been chained to their chairs by Big Malky's henchmen, he'd often come up and lean over them and drop his teeth in their laps. 'Ah'm gauny schuck ye tae death,' he would say. 'Mah gumsch isch regischtered asch lethal weaponsch.' Sometimes he brought along a joke wind-up chattering set for extra effect.

Tad, like many comedians, always used a stooge or victim, someone to be the butt of his humour, and Tad had decided early on that Jim – the biggest of the three boys chained up for him this evening – would be his. Something to do with the innocent look on the boy's face. Tad offered him a banana. Jim looked down at his chained hands and Tad said, 'Oopsch-a-daischy, schilly me, schilly me. Here, Ah'll feed ye, like this look. . . . Not like that, like that.' The boy didn't cry as the banana was peeled and fed too quickly into his mouth – which was good going because many of Tad's victims broke down at this point. Tad, chuckling to himself and saying, 'itsch the way Ah tell em,' decided that he really liked this boy. Then, this being the punchline of his banana routine, he slipped on the discarded skin.

Big Malky wasn't laughing. Big Malky never laughed. Big Malky'd heard all Tad's lines before and was very bored with the banana thing. He looked up now from his copy of *Hello!* magazine – he always brought reading material to these little soirées – and gestured to Tad with his cigarette, mouthing the words 'get on with it.' Or something to that effect.

Tad supposed it was time to start. 'Big man back there schaysch Ah've goat tae get a move oan,' he told Jim. 'Look a' hisch fasche. Mischerable or whit? 'Schlike hisch rabbit drapped deid an he oanly goat a quid fer the hutch. He'sch goat thisch problem wi patschiensch – ye keep him waitin an ye end up in hoaschpital . . . ye know, asch a patschient. Which isch why yousche are here, Ah imagine. Fer keeping him waitin Ah mean. An fer money, which isch the schort of waitin he'sch leascht fond o.'

'Aye,' said Jim.

'Well tell me aboot it, pal,' Tad said. 'Me too. Borrowed a grand, couldnae pay it back, he schaid Ah had tae help him torture people or he'd schtamp oan me.'

'Tha's terrible,' said Jim.

'Aye,' said Tad. 'Ah wischnae exschactly tickled tae death aboot it. But scheriouschly folksch, Ah widnae schay he'sch a bad man, but even his freensch isch schcared of him. An, by the way, schee if he aschksch ye tae come roon fer dinner? Mah advische isch tae schay no, causche ye might be the main coursche. Ye'll be gaein hame minusch a leg or schumpin. Great way tae losche weight, mind. Oanyway, how much ye borrow?'

'Couple a thousand quid,' said Jim. 'Me an the boys here is puttin a band togither.'

'Band?' said Tad. 'A'sch great. Ah alwaysch wanted tae get intae the entertainment buschinesch. Tad'sch mah name, laughin'sch mah game. Ah could ae been a contender, ye know. There wasch people wansche upon a time schaid Ah couldae been the new Norman Wischdom.'

'We needed the cash for gear,' Jim said. 'Sept we didnae get enough gigs so we couldnae pay the guy back.'

'Why did ye no get oany gigsch?' Tad was interested. 'Schay, tell ye whit. Dae ye need a funny wee front man? Ah sching a bit an play the ukelele, ye know. Hing oan there, Ah'll get ma uke, Ah'll gie ye a wee blascht o schumpin. Muschic Mischter Maeschtro pleasche.'

'O we goat gigs,' said Jim as Tad was picking the instrument up off the table and giving it a preparatory strum. 'But no enough. No enough tae pay the equipment an a' that.'

Tad had had an idea of doing either the chorus of 'Bring me Sunshine', or possibly the whole of 'With Me Little Stick of Blackpool Rock' – a song he always managed to perform with far more menace than other entertainers could ever have even dreamed of – but then he glanced round at Big Malky and thought better of it. Big Malky was pulling out the iron bar he always kept in his inside coat pocket.

Tad could see that it was time to bring his act to a close.

'Schorry aboot thisch pal,' he said to Jim, gesturing at Big Malky. 'But Ah've tae get oan wi the buschinesch here. Schee the big guy there? He'sch lookin a tad impaschient, like hisch hoosche isch oan fire an Ah'm tryin tae put it oot wi a leaky cup an there'sch nae watter causche Ah left the tapsch oan all night.'

The boy Jim laughed, and Tad winked at him. He bent down to whisper in the boy's ear.

'Tell ye whit, help usch oot here,' he said. 'Ah've goat tae make the big guy think you're schcared oot o yer schkin. Schokay if Ah juscht talk tae ye like thisch, causche he thinksch Ah'm schcarin ye jischt noo. We can be palsch an he'll never know the differensche, 'schlong asch we make a wee effort. Gauny geesch a wee schcream or schumpthin tae help it along.'

Jim obliged with a terrifying scream. He did not seem to find it difficult. Tad winked at him, and noticed that both of Jim's colleagues were whimpering in their seats. One was in tears. Of course, neither of them knew about the bond that was growing between Tad and their friend, but it would all become clear to them soon.

'A'hm schorry yer in thisch schituation,' Tad told him. 'An Ah mean tha moscht schinscherely, Ah really dae.'

'Sawright,' said Jim. 'Ah wiz expectin much worse when the big guy there an his gorillas picked us up this aifternoon. You're OK, pal. See you an me, we could be freens.'

'Ah feel the schame way. No scheriouschly,' Tad whispered in Jim's ear. 'We're the schame, you an me. Jischt pawnsch in the game, eh?'

'Aye,' Jim agreed, 'a's right.'

'An baith talented too,' Tad said. 'Schee whit ye schaid aboot the band? Ah tried tae make it asch a schtond-up comedian, well, asch schtond-up asch ye can be when yer knee high tae a bloake wi dead schort schinsch, but people schaid they didnae get the joakesch causche they couldnae underschtond whit Ah wasch schayin. An they thought it wasch schtrange bein tellt joakesch by a wee schtumpy freak like maschel.'

Jim smiled, nodding his head in agreement. 'Sterrible. Know jist whit yer sayin,' he said. 'They didnae really understand oor act neither. See oor Davie over there? Writes great songs, dead brilliant, but people just dinnae get them. Could be famous, that boy.'

'Whit,' said Tad. 'A poap schtar?'

'Aye,' said Jim.

'Really?' said Tad.

'Aye,' said Jim.

'An him wi hisch fasche all schcarred an messchy like tha? Like an accschident in a pizzscha factory?'

'Whit're ye talkin aboot?' said Jim. 'His face isnae all scarred.'

'No,' Tad agreed. 'No' yet. But in a minute it wull be.'

Jim looked puzzled. Tad took pity on him. Waving Big Malky back a moment, he explained the situation.

'Ah'm jischt Malky'sch warm-up man,' he said. 'He schaysch it hurtsch ye far moare if ye get tortured by schomewan ye've made friendsch wi causche ye get bewildered. He schaysch torturin an a'sch no really aboot the pain, it'sch all tae dae wi yer emotionsch. He schaysch it'sch like the good cop bad cop thing oan the TV. Ah widnae know. Ah'm jischt the schtooge. He'sch the ecshpert.'

Tad gestured to the man standing behind him.

Big Malky was smiling. A broad one. Ear to ear.

'Oanyway,' Tad continued, 'tha's the end o mah schpot, Ah'm oot ae time. 'Schtime noo tae hond ye over tae the main attractschion o the evenin, the wan an oanly Big Malky. Fore Ah go, can Ah jischt schay Ah think ye've been a lovely audiensche, an Ah really mean tha', Ah really dae. Ah've been Tad Valley, ye've been mairvellousch. Goodnight an, Jim . . . Goad blesch, eh?'

Kathryn Heyman grew up in Australia, where she worked as deckhand, actor and playwright. Her first novel, The Breaking, *was shortlisted for the 1997 Stakis Award for the Scottish Writer of the Year, and long-listed for the 1998 Orange Prize. Her second novel,* Keep Your Hands On the Wheel, *was published by Orion in June 1999. Kathryn lives with her partner and their young daughter, and they divide their time between Edinburgh and Oxford.*

Lowlands

By Kathryn Heyman

Celtic harp, which I've always hated, and you would hate even more if you were here. God, you would hate it so much. I know that, although we never spoke about it. It's a woman playing, with a man on electric piano by her side. Electric piano and Celtic harp. If I listen hard enough, I can hear you laughing at it. Snorting in disgust. Normally, I'd walk away. Normally, I wouldn't even be here, but it's New Year's Day and the gallery is full of bright young things. Twenty-thirties or whatever it is they call us in marketing meetings these days. Like me. Like you. Like you must be, by now. People are all over the place: lying back against walls, huddled alongside each other. We have given up wandering about, eyeing the pictures nervously. It's too crowded, too stuffy and hot, and we've become like small tired children, cuddled up, listening passively. Nursing orange juice or gin or coffee and hangovers. Waiting for the year to begin, to offer something new. And in the mean time, letting the music wash over us, in among the photographs and paintings of odd bits of anatomy.

A super-skinny woman steps over my foot, her too-long flares catch on my boot and she nearly trips. Her hands fly out and her hair flicks back. For a moment – like I always do – I think it's you. It's her hair, long and almost peach-coloured, if hair can be peach-coloured. You'd pick me up on that, I know, give me the range of appropriate terms for hair colour or texture or style. New Year's Day. Ridiculous that you're not here. Andy is leaning on my back, hurting me with the weight of him. I look at him to see if he knows that it's ridiculous but of course he doesn't. How could he? He doesn't even know you.

They're singing some audience interaction song now. Oh I can't believe it. Do you believe it? As if, as if folk are going to open their mouths on New Year's Day and sing some old crofty song. The woman's laid her harp down, she's got her eyes closed and mousy brown hair which you would do something wild and interesting with. She's singing the song and it goes like this: lowlands, lowlands away, my John. We're supposed to sing the lowlands bit back at her – there's a sort of group grunt which forms something roughly resembling a tune for those bits. My mouth isn't even open – I'm not being cynical, it's just that I'm thinking about you, about our picnics. Then she gets to the verse that says something about a dream. A dream she had that you were lost, lost out in the lowlands. Andy puts his hand out for me to hold, he must feel me shaking. He sits up, touches my shoulder, says 'All right?' and he is, even now, further away from me than you are.

Skinny Flares Woman climbs back through all the sprawled-out legs and bodies, holding a tray of drinks in one hand. She steps over me and I want to hit her or yell in her face for having peach hair which flies away like yours. It's not normally like this. Usually, it's okay, it's fine. I mean, I still see you on buses, in shops. Now and then, it lasts for more than a second or two and I run after the bus, the car, the stranger. Very occasionally, I imagine what I'll say when I find you. Sometimes I hate Andy for something, I'm not sure what. Partly for not knowing you, but it's more than that too. I can't grab hold of the something else – it just comes on me. I look at his face and my breath goes and fear shifts in between us. He is so foreign to me then. So, sometimes, not so good. But mostly fine. New Year's Day is always hardest. Because of the picnics.

In my head, in my memory, it's something we always did. Never a time that we didn't start the year with a graveyard picnic. Starting with the dead, starting with some desire to be in the snow, cold and fresh. Always know you're alive when you're cold. You used to say that. When we did the school trip to Spain, you lay in the shade like a queen, waving your hands about, insisting on ice being brought to you. Heat can't kill you, I said, and you laughed like a maniac. *Tell that to those poor lads who died in the Kalahari Desert.* I didn't – still don't – have a clue what lads you meant but Mrs Leproy called out and said Tabitha Simon and Anita Joy, stop behaving like drama queens and get on the bus. Drama queen, you loved that. We sat on the bus, winding around the hills of Ibiza, singing songs from all the musicals we could think of. Being drama queens. The first picnic was that year, after Spain. Your idea, as always. Snow had fallen all through Christmas, right up to Hogmanay. The plum tree in our garden was weighed down with a thick, thick hat of snow. Everything was crisp, fresh. Sleepy, but alive.

First day of the fresh new year, and there you were, kicking at my door, an armful of blankets covering your face. *We have to make the most of the snow.* You had painted a banner, tied bits of coloured suede bunting to it. You stood on the doorstep, calling me to the door so that you could unfurl it like a sail. *Happy New Year, Drama Queen.* Your face, winter-white except for the red dots on your cheeks. The banner flapped around your feet, the word 'Queen' hidden by your legs. My mother fluttered, what she always did best, calling you in for tea, for toast and goodness-me-what-on-earth-is-that? Your Christmas camera – Just What You Always Wanted – dangled around your neck like a pendant, or a noose. *The graveyard looks like Russia, get your boots on, let's go and wake the dead.* I followed you, as always, hauling a basket of crisps, jam pieces, bananas, mince pies, clementines: (Christmas left-overs) and an extra roll of film.

They're all in my album, all the photos, tucked away somewhere safe. Snowmen next to ancient gravestones. My face smiling next to a lump of snow which had once been a rose bush. And you, lying on a tombstone, your arms out, wing-shaped indents in the snow where you'd flapped your arms. *Take this one: call it 'Angel wings'.* Three shots I had to take, with you rearranging your face to make it angelic. As if, Tabitha Simon, you could get an angel pout on to your face.

Lowlands, lowlands away, my John. They are singing along now, more than a grunt, although less than full-throated throttle. *You call to me at night, I hear you, buried in the lowlands.* Andy has his hand on my arm, stroking me up and down like a pet. 'Will you no have a drink, hen?' His face peers at me. Forehead creased. Worried. He sees me disappear like this, he knows the signs and thinks he understands. He doesn't know the half of it, though. Because in these times, what I want is for him to be disappeared. He doesn't know that, doesn't have a clue. You'd like him though, you will, when you come back. You'll kick at the door, regale me with your adventures, then look Andy over and give me the thumbs up. Give him the thumbs up. He's never seen the photos.

Your mum gave me your graduation photo. So tough, you with your blue hair and red lips and plastic skirt. Except for the last-minute doubts. *I'm not going to make it across that stage, Net.* Your mouth tickled my ear. Two feet from the long walk up those steps, the totter across the stage to pick up a wee piece of paper from a fat man in a robe, and you start hyperventilating in my ear. As it was, you managed to do a little twirl for the bored Friends and Families of Graduates. Even the fat old chancellor smiled. Your fear was always smaller than your desire. Laughing. That's the last picture I have of you, a huge spread of laughter wiping across your face, the wind behind you and at your feet. One strand of hair sliced across your eye, cutting your face in two and flapping like a whip. You are there, like this, beside me all the time. Even when I forget you, even when I notice nothing for days except my own happiness. Days of being wound up in that Spring smell, the smell of hope, get paused suddenly by that picture of you. I'm in the picture too, standing on the doorstep, calling to you in the dark.

Andy's breath is light on me, I can smell coffee and woodsmoke on him. He's familiar and warm and safe but when he breathes in my ear, says: 'You want home?', I want to smash him. Why would that be, do you think, Tabitha? Why would I be so damned angry with him? He planted me a plum bush for Christmas, spent days putting decorations up, cooked a turkey roast that even had my mum going. Complete with stuffing. Mum keeps asking when will we get married, when? Desperate for grand-children, of course, you know what she's like. I imagine you looking her in the eye and saying: Anita can't get married, Mrs Joy, she has a rare disease that makes it impossible for her to eat wedding cake without vomiting over the nearest man in a tuxedo. All the time, these words in your head, in my head. Until I'm not sure which is which. When I get dressed, you sit on my bed behind me, saying 'you can't wear those trousers, they make you look like a schoolteacher.' Even now, you have an opinion on everything in my life.

What I tell mum is that Andy and I don't need to get married, we already have a commitment, a piece of paper won't change it, and so on, and so on. I tell Andy the same, and add that it would make us stale, old. Truth is, I'd love to get married. But who will be my Best Woman if you don't come back, Tab? Your mum used to say: 'Maybe she joined a circus, she loved animals. Or the Hare Krishnas. For the singing.' Always hoping, holding out for the best. Haven't seen her, your mum, for a few years. Christmas cards get sent back and forth; mine say: *Merry Christmas, Mrs S. Can't believe it's that time already! All is well here, hope it is with you. Love, Anita and Andy.* Or: *Must get to see you this year.* Hers say: *Dear Anita, A peaceful New Year to you. Love, Ruby Simon.* One year, early on, she wrote: *Still no news from our Tabby; we're all missing her dreadfully.* Once, in Spain of all places, I heard a loud laugh like a shriek and I knew it was you. Don't know why you'd be in Spain with all that heat, but I know it was you. Andy and I spent the whole day wandering the streets, searching.

The musicians are winding up, selling CDs, sending punters downstairs to the bar. There's a swarm of suddenly active potential drunks climbing over me. Andy grabs my hand and says, 'Let's have a look at the gallery.' I say, 'Yes, okay,' even though I'm bored. Bored with being here, bored with the music, with you and your absence. Bored with this damned new year already. With waiting for you, for some sign. Maybe I'm just tired, just hungover. We spent the night shivering in Princes Street, waiting for something to happen. When the fireworks burst out over the castle, I felt my body, my whole self, full of rush. Full of everything. Andy stood behind me with his hands on my hips and I could have swallowed him whole, that's how much I wanted him. Today, though, the day after last night, I do not want his hand grabbing at me, I do not want his concern for my memory.

You're standing on my doorstep, the dark behind you, the wind grabbing at your clothes. You're lit up by the spill from the hallway, the light shifts on your face. You wave an envelope in the air, like victory, like success. The wind is so loud behind you that I can barely hear your words, flying at me from the night. *I hope they accept me.* Your face is streaked with excitement, you know they will accept you, you with your glorious First. Your hair is lashing your face in the wind; now I see you, now I don't. My mum's voice comes from behind me, but it's you she's calling to, not me. *Be careful walking back, Tabitha. In fact, why don't I get Ralph to drive you? Ralph?* We suck our cheeks in, roll our eyes at each other, yell at the nagging worrier not to worry, to leave it be. I wag my finger at you, say: 'You never know who you'll meet out there, could be a loony.' You giggle and say, *Could be Mister Right, though. You never know.*

And you never do know. It could have been anyone you met that night, it could have been any man, it could have been no one. The application wasn't posted but who knows? I wait, and wait, and wait. Listening for edges of laughter, looking in cold places for women with your hair. Reading endless bloody stories of another woman found, another man arrested, another case solved. There was one this week; body after body after body carried out from the earth, a bearded man hiding his face from the camera. Details yet to be confirmed, and so on.

Andy's arm slips around my waist and I let myself lean against him. It could have been anyone; it could have been no one; it could have been him. He whispers 'Happy New Year, hen' and I smile and pass it on to you. Happy New Year, Drama Queen.

Maybe this year, you'll come home.

Susie Maguire is a writer and actor, who has also worked as a stand-up and television presenter. She is co-editor of Something Wicked *and two previous Polygon anthologies,* Scottish Love Stories *and* HOOTS! Scottish Comic Writing. *Many of her stories have been produced for radio, and her play,* Split Ends, *about the glamorous world of Scottish hairdressing, was broadcast on Radio 4 in December 1998. She lives in Edinburgh.*

Statutes and Judgements

By Susie Maguire

There are twenty-three possible D. Christies in the phone book. I exclude the dozen who live too far outside the city centre to commute, and the ones who give their full names. The one I'm looking for doesn't volunteer information. Of course, some of those Ds might be discreet Dianes, Doreens, Dorothies. Pulling out a city map, I circle the areas corresponding to the telephone exchanges. Should I call every one of the twenty-three, or find some other way to narrow down the search?

I know his work number off by heart now, and call the switchboard.

'Can you tell me what time you stop work?'

'Which department were you wanting?'

'It doesn't matter, could you just tell me when everyone leaves the building?'

The woman sighs.

'You'll not get anyone at their desk after 4.30, dear, and it's nearly that now . . .'

I grab coat, scarf, keys, and run down the four flights to the street. The building is only a couple of blocks away; if I'm quick I might spot him leaving. Which exit will he use? If I stand half-way down the street, in the doorway of the closed sandwich shop, I'll be unobserved and still have a fair chance of seeing any sign of mass exodus. Just as I reach the shop it starts to rain, and I'm glad of the excuse it gives me to cover my hair with the scarf. The street is quiet. Next door, the proprietor of a second-hand TV shop stares out into the darkening sky. From my doorway I see children's programmes on five sets in his window, racing on two more. It looks sunny in England.

A trickle emerges from the mouth of the office complex and becomes a stream of moving people, umbrellas blooming instantly in the warm rain. I press further back into the doorway, as groups of men and women, hunching shoulders and tugging at their collars, straggle past. What will he be wearing? I saw only his face and upper body at the interview. Green shirt, straggly brown hair, a full mouth, strong nose, eyes partially hidden behind tinted lenses in a silver frame. I look for someone with glasses and a cigarette, remembering my fear as I'd watched his tobacco-stained fingers flick through my dossier only a few hours ago.

Department of Social Security is a misnomer. Let's call it something real, let's call it Department of 'Just Doing My Job'. Waiting, in the sweat-scented smoky anteroom, I'd run through a dozen alternatives, lyrics to the rhythm of my pounding heartbeat. I'd felt as though I were running a fast mile sitting still, anticipation drying my mouth and throat, head full of parts of sentences, a jumble of half-truths and excuses. Not knowing what I'd done wrong, but suspecting that my own habitual guilt would condemn me if I let it show, was no frame of mind in which to be interrogated.

The sun emerges weakly, causing an incongruous rainbow to appear in the leaden sky, low over the huge concrete DSS monolith. My mouth twists at the irony. Pot of Gold. The State Will Provide. To Him That Hath Shall Be Given. While I think my thoughts, the flood dries up, people grouped in puddles at bus-stops evaporate. I've missed him, just as well perhaps. Wait. Two men come through the reception area, pausing to exchange a joke with the guard at the door. Both wear padded nylon jackets and have dark hair. The smaller might be D. Christie. They leave together, walking uphill, and I follow at some distance. The taller man stops outside a pub, inclines his head. The possible D. Christie shakes his head, waves goodbye, starts back down the street.

When he passes, I catch the reflection in a window, superimposed on a clutter of surfboards and neon-bright wet-suits, the glint of his spectacles, hand to mouth, inhaling smoke. The smell of hot cigarette lingers behind him like a fart. Now he's moving with speed, checking the time, and I'm sure it's him, the set of his head, even the back of it, producing a sensation in the pit of my stomach that is recognition. He crosses the road, glancing at traffic, running a little to reach the pavement before the approaching taxi barrels past. Delayed by several more vehicles, I lose sight of him for a moment, and walk the length of the street twice, anxiously scanning, until I practically hug him as he emerges from a small delicatessen. I dip my head and enter the shop he has just left, pause for a few beats and leave, to see him stuff a pint of milk into one pocket of his jacket, a battered paper bag containing white floury rolls into the other.

He leans flat against the wall by a bus-stop, and I have nowhere to hide. In panic I search my pockets for props and come upon sunglasses, a little pretentious but good enough as a disguise. Self-consciously aware of my sudden resemblance to Françoise Dorléac, I too lean, casually, against the wall, sneaking glances at my quarry from behind the dusty brown lenses. He smokes a Gauloise. D. Christie as Yves Montand. D. Christie as Eddie Constantine. Will he suddenly break into song? Get Marcel Carné in here to direct this and we could have accordion music and a happy ending. My fantasy is arrested by the arrival of a bus.

He gives me no more than a brief once-over as he merges with the head of the queue. I smile to myself, acknowledging that this lack of recognition reflects his attitude to his work, to me. I push a bit to get close enough to eavesdrop on his fare, then take a seat two back and across the aisle. I re-assess my victim.

Item: the label from his maroon jacket sticks up at the back.
Item: he has dandruff on his collar, hair that needs cutting.

Item: he has just surreptitiously picked his nose, inspected the result
and wiped it on the seat.
Item: he is whistling through his teeth, and the tune is undoubtedly
Robert Palmer's most recent macho anthem.

These things are sufficient, with what I know of him, to reinforce my
instinct for retribution.

Where is he going? The bus enters a part of the city with which I am
unfamiliar, passes shops selling shoddy goods, three for a pound, brand
names too obscure to boast about. For a moment I'm on holiday, a tourist
abroad without fixed agenda, free to take pleasure in the strangeness of my
journey, the little frisson that comes of adventuring beyond known
territory. The weak evening sun is almost hot through the glass. I turn
into it, warming my face, gazing out without focus. There is a stillness now
in my head, replacing the tinnitus of fear. It would be the most pleasant
thing in the world to go on forever riding round and round in this bus, in
constant suspension of time. I could almost forget.

I think again of the letter, the bold signature under 'p.p. Area Manager',
the confident officialese. During the interview he'd told me he was just
doing his job, it was nothing personal, and I'd believed it, believed there
was no plea I could make that would alter the finality of his decision. The
finality of his green shirt, his big mouth. The stubby spatulate fingers,
yellow and brown in places from his disgusting habit. The form I'd refused
to sign. Moral right versus legal right. He hadn't understood. That shake of
the head, pursing of lips, was he Pontius Pilate in a former life? Just doing
his job. What kind of security does that imply?

The seat behind D. Christie becomes vacant and I move into it. I count
the moles on the back of his neck, note the shape of his ears, the thinning
hair at the crown of his head, inhale and exhale in his rhythm, wondering
that he does not sense our closeness, that he shows no intuitive qualities.
Part of the contract of employment. Give up your sixth sense at the door,
sign here, you can have it back with your enhanced Civil Service pension
and gold-plated carriage-clock when we're eventually privatised or you're
made redundant, whichever comes first. D. Christie, on the dole. How
would he manage on £44 a week? How would he manage if they took even
that away from him? Suspension. Suspension of life.

He gets up. The bus swings wide round a corner, accelerates to a stop,

causing passengers' knuckles to whiten as they grip seat-backs. I tag after
him down a street of grimy stone tenements, testament to the city's log-
jam of housing repairs. The pavement is strewn with refuse, fag ends, crisp
packets, and a child's sugar-pink scooter lies abandoned in the gutter
outside number 14, which D. Christie enters. I walk past, return on the
other side of the road, using the phone box as a hide. A light goes on in the
top flat, behind short orange curtains. Projecting from the window is a For
Sale sign, the agent's number too small and too distant to read. It is
gratifying to find a phone book still in reasonable condition. D. Christie,
14 Eskbank Dr. I need to re-acquaint myself with his voice, to torment him
a little.

'Hello, is this the flat for sale?' I have watched enough Brookside to be
sure my accent is passable.

'Er, yes, yes it is, actually, yeah.'

'Would it be possible to see the flat this evening, like?'

'Er, well I'm what time would you be wanting?'

'Sorry, the thing is, I'm waiting on my husband getting back, he works
late on a Thursday. Would about 10.15 be okay?'

'You couldn't make it Sunday, could you?'

'Oh, I know my husband's very keen, he said it's right where we want to
be, top flat and everything, I mean we'd be looking to make an offer
tomorrow if we liked it, so . . .'

'Right, right, well okay then, some time after 10, and the name is?'

'Er, Lennon, Mr and Mrs Lennon. Thanks.'

He doesn't question the direct call instead of a viewing through his
estate agents, must be desperate to sell. In the dying light, I look at the dirty
street, the neglected patches of garden, and don't blame him for that.

In all my anger and frustration, my desire for revenge, I have thought
no further than this point. I know where he lives – and now what? Until
something has been resolved I will not entertain the safe, sensible
alternatives – forgetting the whole thing, buying a bag of chips and
spending the evening, and probably the rest of my life, in front of the TV.
I will not plan to return another day. Spontaneity, long diminished by the
restrictions my income has placed on my expectations, fuel me now to do
something extraordinary. I desire to impede the course of D. Christie's
life as abruptly as he has altered mine. And the train of events, finding
him, following him, confirming my judgement on him, are all falling into

place so beautifully. Never put off until tomorrow what you can do today.

A gas leak? A flood? Report of a suicide attempt? These things are too transient, simply inconvenient to have to explain to the emergency services. How angry do I feel?

Scroll back three months. I'm standing in a dark street, not unlike this one, looking up at a window. Inside a couple dance, kiss, laugh. I have known the man intimately during the past eighteen months. Since then I have stood here often in the dark, replaying in my head the final scene between us: my tears, his coldness. My pleas, his judgement. All he'd left behind was a sock under the bed. The letters returned unopened. At times I'd lain in wait for him, followed him, suffered his fury, his verdict that I behaved like a victim, that I was insane, that I wouldn't accept the truth if . it slapped me in the face. He had a strong face, a strong personality, so strong he sucked away my confidence and left me weak. Too weak to be angry. Then.

Outside the smelly phone box night is falling rapidly, and beneath the sodium lighting the street looks a perfect setting for crime. At the far end the light is stronger, for there are shops, a pub, a chippy and a Chinese takeaway. Here, by D. Christie's house, the light is poor. I cross the street and enter the stair. At the back of the building a passage leads into a communal drying green. I climb to the brightly lit first landing. Upper floors have been seen to by previous vandals, but the light here is functioning, despite the dents and cracks. Removing my shoe, I whack at the plastic two, three, four times, hard enough to disturb the filament and put it out of order. In a cold sweat, I expect the hand on the shoulder, the shout through the letter box, but compared to 'Top of the Pops' it has made hardly a sound. The stair is quite dark now. I go up and pause for a while outside D. Christie's door, putting my ear to the letter flap. Television, advertising jingles.

I return to the passage and sit on an empty crate. It's a gamble; if he doesn't leave the flat a frontal approach will have to be devised. But I have confidence in my assessment of his character. In fact I feel almost happy. After the waiting game, the interview, the fear, action is more than a relief. Perhaps there's something in voluntary work after all.

I examine the contents of my pockets. Tissues, three bus tickets, keys, purse. The sunglasses, a brooch with a broken pin. I find two Polo mints and divide my rations, one now, one for later. I count how long it takes on one side of my mouth for the molar to react to the sugar, then switch to the opposite cheek and count again. Attempting to recall in detail every check-up since I lost my milk teeth occupies me for a while.

My backside is growing numb when I hear movement on the stair. Footsteps descending, a voice cursing the lack of vision. The faint silhouette as the person steps on to the street has me on my feet and following. I know those ears, that walk. My quarry makes straight for his local. The cheap velvet curtains afford me glimpses of the interior, and I am pleased to see him greeted with a nod by the barman, hailed by couples at a corner table. He takes his pint across the room to join them. Above the bar, a clock reads 7.52 pm. I feel safe in assuming he'll be there until close on ten. In two hours I can surely find what I need.

In fact it takes only minutes to find a skip, to reach in and arm myself. I hide my prizes in a doorway while I backtrack to the corner shop to get a samosa, then take my supper and my other valuables back to D. Christie's tenement. The hours pass, slowly, time black as pitch, black as coal. I can just about see my own hands, down here in the murk, gnawing my vittles. I am nervous, as I had been before the interview, dry mouth, sweating palms, racing pulse. Waiting again, my old enemy.

Soon it is quiet on the street. Not much of a moon. About now D. Christie will be taking his leave of the Old Bellevue Bar, grinding his last Gauloise to ash, the premature sale celebration flooding him with good cheer. He'll come back needing a slash, and hoping to give the air time to clear in the toilet before his potential buyers ring the doorbell. Maybe a wee cup of coffee before they arrive, to cut the smell of beer and sober up a little. Not that he needs it, he can hold his drink with the best of them, D. Christie. He whistles something or other the pub band played, on the tip of his tongue, come on, it's a standard. Nah, it's gone. Fuck, this stair's dark.

He starts up the first flight, unaware of his shadow. When he reaches the landing his shadow flattens to the wall until he grabs the bannister and hauls himself up toward the next floor. Too many fags, D. Christie. The shadow takes on a curious shape as it slides after him, its hands engaging in some sort of puppet-dance of manipulation. Half-way up the penultimate flight he gets dizzy, pauses for breath, leaning his head against the cool, scarred wood of the bannister. Perfect.

The brick hits him at the nape of the neck, just where his hair starts to fuzz and grow down on to his shoulders. It makes a soft clunk, echoed by the whoosh of air as he gasps, trying to lift his head. His hands still grip the wood, he's leaning away from me, each foot twisting on its toes, arching his back against the railings, but he doesn't really want to see because he raises one hand to his eyes. Chicken. I grasp his knees and pull up, so that his hip slides on to the bannister, then he's on his back, hands flailing. He doesn't offer much resistance, or maybe I'm too quick for him, too efficient.

Will I, won't I? I tuck his feet under my elbows, his legs are stiff, straight beneath my breasts, it's just like playing wheelbarrows. Here goes. One good hard shove. His knuckles rattle the railings on the way down, and a faint whisper, a question, issues from his lungs before he hits the concrete. What did you want to say, D. Christie? Why? Why me?

Silence. Nobody cracks open a door to shed light on the situation, nobody pursues a neighbourly impulse to see if all is as it should be at 14 Eskbank Drive. A religious addiction to 'Taggart' holds them in thrall. Nothing like crime to keep you in your seat. I look down into the stairwell but can discern no movement. Picking up my brick, I start down.

He lies on his back, looking strangely soft and boneless, a flounder. I am not indifferent to his fate. I wouldn't say I was indifferent. A great one for following through, completing the task, tying up loose ends. So despite the need for caution, I move closer. His eyes are closed but flickering. A tiny noise in his throat alerts me. I bend over him just enough to hear, if he should speak. One word. 'Lennon.'

The walk home is long, the night has turned chill. I concentrate on keeping the final Polo away from my molars. On the principles of 'The Purloined Letter', I chuck the brick into a skip in a housing action area, where it looks just like any other brick. If bricks could talk, I think, dusting off my hands, what would this one cry out?

D. Christie didn't cry out. D. Christie was not a man to volunteer information.

Val McDermid grew up in a Scottish mining community and attended Oxford University. After working as a journalist for fourteen years, she turned to full-time writing. Her mystery novel, The Mermaids Singing, won Britain's prestigious Crime Writers Association Golden Dagger Award for Best Crime Novel of 1995 and Crack Down was shortlisted for a 1995 Anthony Award.

The Writing on the Wall

By Val McDermid

I've never written anything on a toilet wall before, but I don't know what else to do. Please help me. My boyfriend is violent towards me. He batters me and I don't know where to turn.

KICK THE BASTARD WHERE IT HURTS. GIVE HIM A TASTE OF HIS OWN MEDICINE.

> Get out of the relationship now before he does you serious injury. Battering men only batter with our consent.

I can't believe these responses. I asked for help, not a lecture. I love him, don't you realise that? He was raped and battered as a child. Are we just supposed to ignore damaged people?

IF YOU DON'T GET OUT OF THE RELATIONSHIP, THEN YOU'RE GOING TO END UP ANOTHER ONE OF THE DAMAGED PEOPLE. AND WHO WILL HELP YOU THEN?

Ask your friends for their support in dealing with him. When his violence begins, leave the house and go and stay with a friend.

I can't walk out on him. He needs me. And I can't tell my friends because I'm too ashamed to admit to them that I'm in a relationship with a man who batters me.

Sooner or later they're going to notice, and then they're going to feel angry that you've excluded them from something so important.

How come you're the one who's ashamed, not him? He's the one dishing out the violence, after all.

LIKE I SAID AT THE START, FIGHT BACK. LET HIM KNOW WHAT BEING HIT FEELS LIKE.

He knows what being hurt feels like. He spent his childhood being hurt. And he is ashamed of his violence. He hates himself for his behaviour, and he's always really sorry afterwards.

WELL, WHOOPEE SHIT! THAT MUST REALLY HELP YOUR BRUISES!

This is the first time I've been in this loo, and I can't believe how unsupportive you're all being to this woman! Sister, there is counselling available. You deserve help; there's a number for the confidential helpline in the student handbook. Use it, please.

It's not just you that needs counselling. Tell your boyfriend that unless he comes for counselling with you, you will leave him. If he refuses, then you know his apologies aren't worth a toss.

> Leave him; tell him you'll only take him back once he has had counselling and learned to deal with his problem in a way that doesn't include violence. Anything else is a betrayal of all the other women who get battered every day.

Thanks for the suggestion. I've phoned the helpline and we're both going to meet the counsellor next week.

> I still say leave him till he's got himself sorted out. He's only going to end up resenting you for making him go through all this shit.

I'M GLAD YOU'VE TAKEN THIS STEP FORWARD; LET US KNOW HOW YOU GO ON.

Sorry it's taken me so long to get back to you all. My lectures were moved out of this building for a couple of weeks because of the ceiling collapse. We've had three joint counselling sessions so far, and I really feel that things are getting better!

YOU MEAN HE ONLY BATTERS YOU ONCE A WEEK INSTEAD OF EVERY NIGHT?

> Now he's made the first step, you can tell him you're going to move out till the course of counselling has finished. You owe it to yourself and to the other victimised women out there to show this batterer that he is no longer in a position of control and power over you.

> *Well done. Good luck.*

I'm not moving out on him. I'm going to stick with him because he's trying so hard. He's really making the effort to deal with his anger and to resolve the conflicts that make him lash out at me. I love him; everybody seems to keep forgetting that. If you love somebody, you want to help them get better, not abandon them because they're not perfect.

ANSWER THE QUESTION, IS HE STILL HITTING YOU?

Oh for God's sake, leave her alone. Can't you see she's having enough of a struggle helping the guy she loves without having the holier-than-thou tendency on her back?

> Save us from the bleeding hearts. If he's still hitting her, she's still collaborating with his oppressive behaviour. She should walk away while she can still walk.

So where's she supposed to go? A women's refuge packed with damaged kids and mothers isn't exactly the ideal place to study, is it?

ANYWHERE'S GOT TO BE BETTER THAN A PLACE WHERE YOU GET HURT CONSTANTLY.

And you think battering someone is the only way to hurt them? Grow up!

He hasn't hit me for over a week now. He's made a real breakthrough. He has contacted his mother for the first time in three years and confronted her with the abuse he experienced from his stepfather. He says he feels like he's released so much pressure just by telling her about it.

SURPRISE, SURPRISE. NOW HE'S FOUND A WOMAN TO BLAME, HE'S GOING TO BE ALL RIGHT.

Yeah, how come he hasn't confronted the abuser? How come he has to offload his guilt on his poor bloody mother who was probably battered too?

Leave him. You are perpetuating the circle of violence. He will see your forgiveness as condoning his behaviour. Break out. Now. If you stay, you are as bad as he is.

Don't listen to them. Stick with him. You are making progress. People can change.

Bollocks. Been there, done that, got the bruises. Men who abuse do it because they like it, not because of some behaviour pattern they can change as easily as giving up smoking. The only way to stop being the victim of abuse is to walk away.

He is making changes, I know he is. It's not easy for him, and sometimes it feels like he hates me because I'm the one who persuaded him to confront his problems. He's started to get really jealous and suspicious, even following me to lectures sometimes. He's convinced that because I suggested the counselling. I'm seeing some women's group that is trying to talk me into leaving him. If he only knew the truth! Are there any women out there who have been through this, who would be prepared to do some one-to-one counselling with me?

AH, THE POWER OF THE SISTERHOOD OF THE TOILET WALL! HE'S RIGHT, THOUGH, ISN'T HE? WE ARE TRYING TO MAKE YOU SEE SENSE AND GET OUT OF THIS DESTRUCTIVE RELATIONSHIP.

sounds like you're swapping one problem for another. The guy is major league bad news. sometimes if you love people the best thing you can do for them is to leave them.

I know what you're going through. I'll meet you on Saturday morning on the Kelvin walkway under the Queen Margaret Bridge at 10.30. Come alone. Make sure he's not with you. I'll be watching. If you can't make this Saturday, I'll be there every week till you can.

From the *Scottish Sunday Dispatch:*

Body Found in River Kelvin

Police launched a murder hunt last night after the battered body of a woman student was found floating in the River Kelvin.

A woman walking her dog on the river walkway near Kelvinbridge spotted the body tangled in the roots of a tree.

Police revealed that the victim, who was fully dressed, had been beaten about the head before being thrown in the river.

The woman, whose name is not being released until her family can be contacted, was a second-year biochemistry student at Glasgow University.

Police are appealing for witnesses who may have seen the woman and her attacker on the Kelvin walkway upstream of Kelvinbridge earlier yesterday.

A spokeswoman for the Students' Union said last night, 'This is a terrible tragedy. When a woman gets killed in broad daylight in a public place, you start wondering if there is anywhere that is safe for us to be.'

Duncan McLean was born in Aberdeenshire in 1964 but has lived in Orkney for quite a few years. He has written stories, novels, plays and a musical travelogue, Lone Star Swing. *When the moon is full, he sings with Orkney's leading Western Swing combo,* The Smoking Stone Band.

Shoebox

By Duncan McLean

He said, 'What do you think about when we're having sex?'

'What do you mean?'

'I mean, when we're having sex, what do you think about?'

She looked into space for a few seconds. 'Nothing. I don't think about anything.'

'Nothing? Come on!'

'No, honestly, I don't. I don't think you're meant to think, I think it's more of a feeling thing. I mean if you were thinking about something, you couldn't really be enjoying yourself very much, could you?' She scratched herself somewhere under the covers, then nodded. 'Yes, I would say it's a bad thing to be thinking during sex.'

'Oh aye?'

'Aye.'

'Hih. So why were you smiling back then?'

'When?'

He turned over towards her, propped his head up, looked at her. 'Back then, when I first asked you.'

'I wasn't smiling!'

'Aye you were, I saw you! Jesus, your thoughts must've been pretty dirty before you could smile like that; you were just about drooling over the sheets!'

She rolled her eyes. 'That's cause I'm starving,' she said. 'Away and make some breakfast.'

'What, me?' He sat up. 'Me, the man of the house doing the cooking? Up and do it yourself woman; what else are you good for?'

'Fuck off!' She lay back with her hands behind her head on the pillow. 'What else are *you* good for? Not much, judging by last night's performance.'

'Huh!' He slid out from under the blankets and walked round to the end of the bed, where he started pulling his clothes out of the tangled pile lying there. After a while he said, 'That's not what you were saying last night.'

'I don't remember saying anything last night.'

'Well, that says it all, doesn't it?' He pulled on his T-shirt and tucked it into his jeans, grinning down at her.

'Well, if it makes you happy to think that.'

'Hmm. And what would make you happy, like?'

'Getting some breakfast before I starve to death!' She flung her arms out across the bed and sucked her cheeks in, eyes crossed.

He laughed. 'Two minutes, okay, and I'll get it.' He stuck his feet into his trainers and went over to the door; as he paused to take it off the snib he said, 'Hey, shove on Radio Forth and we can listen to the phone-in show while we're eating.' She yawned in reply, and he went out the door and shut it behind him. His footsteps went away down the corridor towards the toilet.

A couple of minutes later, the door opened again and he stepped in. She was still lying in bed, her back to him; the radio wasn't on. 'Hey,' he said.

She rolled over, looked at him. 'What?'

'Mystical sights in the lavvy!'

'What?'

He went over and sat down on the bed. 'Well, I was standing there having a pee, right, as you do.'

'No I don't.'

'You're just a lazy bugger though. Anyway, you ken how somebody's put in one of those blue rinse things? Well, I was standing there, and I was looking down at this blue water in the pan, and my yellow stuff going into it, and I suddenly thought: Jesus, this looks just like the Northern Lights.'

'Whaaat?'

'I ken, amazing, eh? The pee was going in, and you could see it going in yellowish, and then it would sort of fall down, it would turn greenish and it would fall down through the blue water in short of sheets, no, curtains, greeny curtains waving about and shimmering. Aye, that's how it was. And I tell you, it was just like the Northern Lights: beautiful!'

She had propped herself up on one elbow. 'What a load of shite!'

'No! That would've ruined the effect completely!'

She sighed, blinking slowly. 'Anyway, how do you ken what the Northern Lights look like? You've never seen them.'

'Aye I have.'

'No you haven't.'

'Ah, you're forgetting where I was born and raised, quine. I saw them hundreds of times when I was a kid. We watched them instead of having a telly, in fact.'

She laughed, fell back on the bed.

'Well, I saw them a few times,' he went on. 'And they looked just like that there; made me feel quite nostalgic in fact. They call them the heavenly dancers.'

'Aberdeen,' she called out over his singing. 'The biggest public pisspot in the country.'

He stopped the song. 'You insult my place of birth,' he said, putting on an offended look. 'I'm afraid I must ask you to step outside and . . . make the toast.'

She rolled out of bed and began to get dressed. 'Okay,' she said. 'But only cause I'm wasting away here waiting for you to do it.'

'Why else?'

She smiled at him, stuck up two fingers and left the room.

He listened to her walking away, then laughed to himself and lay back across the bed, putting his hands behind his head as she had done earlier and laughing again. Then he sighed, smiling.

The door banged open and she strode into the room. 'Shit! There's no milk!'

'So?' He sat up. 'We've had it black before.'

'There's no bread either.'

'What? There were at least two slices there last night! Has somebody nicked it? I wouldn't put it past that bastard next door.'

'No, shut up, listen. It's mouldy, that's all.'

He shrugged. 'Cut the bad bits off then.'

'It's all fucking bad bits!' she shouted. 'If I cut the bad bits off we'll be left with two toasted crumbs for our Sunday breakfast!'

He creased his forehead. 'What've we got then?'

She leaned back against the wall, her eyes closed. 'Some lentils.'

'And?'

'That's about it really. There's that Chinese seaweed you bought. Pity you hadn't bought some kippers instead. Mind you, they'd smell pretty bad by now seeing as you've had the bloody stuff for six months and never used it once.'

'I'm just waiting to find a recipe,' he said quietly.

'Aye, okay, okay. But meanwhile could you think up some way to get our breakfast out of lentils, seaweed and scrapings off the floor?'

He thought for a moment, then, 'Couldn't we borrow something from somebody else's cupboard? They wouldn't miss a couple of slices and a wee bit of cheese.'

'What's this? Two seconds ago you were ready to strangle him next door for taking two mouldy heels, and now you're away to nick bread off of him!' She looked down at her feet. 'Anyway, he doesn't have any, I already checked.'

'Ach . . . shite.' He sighed, shook his head and slowly looked up at her. 'We'll have to go across to the shop,' he said at last.

She cleared her throat. 'Aye, I suppose so.'

He got up off the bed, and slowly walked over and out the door. She picked up her coat and followed him: down the corridor and out the flat door into the stair, down two nights then out on to the street, across the cobbled roadway and on to the pavement in front of Majid's.

'You get the milk,' she said. They went in.

He made his way to the counter, squeezing an orange in a tray of fruit on top of the freezer as he passed. There was a groan from the back shop, and the sound of a heavy body struggling up from a spring-busted armchair.

'Morning, Mr Majid,' he called out.

Mr Majid appeared through the bead-curtain behind his counter. 'Oh hello,' he said. 'It's you.'

'Well, it was the last time I looked.'

Mr Majid lifted the corners of his mouth slightly, reached under the counter and brought out a pack of B&H and a box of matches. He lit a fag, inhaled on it deeply, coughed.

'Nasty habit,' the boy said.

Mr Majid coughed again. 'At least I get them wholesale.' The boy laughed. Mr Majid looked at him for a few seconds then said, 'So what can I do you for?'

The boy bent down to the side of the counter and picked up a pint of milk from the crate there.

'Thirty-three,' said Mr Majid.

'And have you got any matches?'

'Wee box?'

'Aye, do fine.' A box of Bluebells was put down beside the milk. 'How much is that so far?'

'Forty-three.'

The boy took money out of his pocket, dumped it on the counter, and slid the coins across to Mr Majid as he counted: 'Twenty, five, five, ten, one, one, one.' He looked at what he was left with. 'What have you got for seventeen?' Mr Majid shrugged, waved his non-smoking hand around the shop. The boy looked at the shelves that went as high as the ceiling, the boxes of fruit and veg ranged along the bottom of them, and the freezer units and sweet display-racks in the middle of the floor. The girl was pottering about by the babyfoods. The boy shouted over his shoulder, 'What do you want for seventeen pence?'

'I don't know,' she replied. 'Something chocolate.'

'A Mars bar, Mr Majid?'

'Twenty.'

'Two Milky Ways?'

'Ten each.'

'A Twix then?'

He took a long drag, looking at the boy over the top of his specs. 'Nineteen,' he said.

'Not seventeen?'

He blew out a jet of smoke. 'Okay, you can owe me.'

'Ach, that's great,' said the boy. 'Ta very much.'

'The next time you're in . . .'

'Aye, sure thing,' said the boy, picking up the milk, matches and Twix.

The girl opened the shop door and called, 'Bye for now,' as she went out. The boy started to walk after her.

Mr Majid stubbed his fag out under the counter somewhere. 'Have a nice day,' he said and, as the boy left the shop, went back through the bead curtain.

Outside, the girl was already on the other pavement, looking back, waiting for the boy. He crossed over to her slowly, and as he caught up with her she headed for their stair door. Once inside, they let it swing to behind them, then immediately they ran: along the passageway, up both flights of stairs, through the flat door, down the corridor and into their room. She collapsed on the bed, him on the floor, and they were both laughing away, gasping for breath in between. After half a minute they calmed down.

'Well,' he said. 'What did you get?'

She sat up on the bed and started pulling things out of the pockets of her coat. Streaky bacon, marge, half a dozen eggs . . .

'Eggs! Jesus, how did you manage them?'

'I have my methods. Now then: tin of tuna, beans . . . hold on, what's this? Processed peas? Shit, I meant to get beans; must've picked up the wrong tin.'

'Never mind, never mind. Anything else? I mean did you get bread or anything?'

She reached inside her coat and from under her arm pulled out a small brown loaf. She held it up to him on the palms of her hands, grinning.

'Brilliant,' he said. 'High in fibre. Health-conscious even now.'

'That little extra for quality goods is always worth it.'

'Little extra? Jesus, did you see that? Thirty-three for a pint of milk; it's criminal!' He slapped his hand down on the floor.

'Ha! He probably has to put his prices up to cover for the amount of stuff folk thieve off him.'

'What, so if I took all this back he'd give me the milk for thirty? Right away!'

'Well, this is where my theory falls down . . .' She flopped out on her back. He leant forward, grabbed her ankles and started to pull her off the bed. She laughed. 'Let go! Mind the eggs!'

He stopped pulling. '*My* theory is,' he said, 'you should go and get started on a big pan of scrambled eggs, I'll stick the bacon under the grill, then we'll stuff our faces with that and have the Twix for pudding. What do you reckon?'

'I reckon barrie. And still, say, tuna sandwiches for tea.'

'Or maybe we could save the tuna for tomorrow? I mean we'll be all right on Tuesday, we'll be able to stock up then.'

'Stock up?' she said. 'To hell with that! Let's just go out somewhere, that Chinese place by the Playhouse, it's good and dear. We'll spend the fucking lot, eat till we can't stuff another crumb down!'

'Eat the whole eighty quid? Impossible: we'd explode!'

'Well, if there was anything left, we'd leave a tip.'

'Ha, tips! Jesus aye! And a taxi home. And live off our fat for a fortnight.'

They laughed for a moment, her sitting on the edge of the bed, him kneeling in front of her. Suddenly she slid down and on to her knees too, put her head in his lap, circled her arms round the bottom of his back; she wasn't laughing any more. She was whispering something, her jaw clenched. 'Jesus, Jesus, Jesus.' She jerked against his body. She was shaking.

After a few seconds he started stroking her hair. Then he stopped and gazed down at her. 'Do you want to know what I think about when we're having sex?' he said.

'Jesus . . .' She sniffed, nodded her head against his leg. Okay.

He stroked her hair with one hand again, the other resting on the small of her back, fingertips under the top of her jeans. 'I don't suppose I do think things really; it's more like I see them. Like sometimes I see myself sort of flying, no, more like bouncing: leaping about over the city. It's night, and there are lights in the windows, but I'm outside. And I'm floating about above it all. I land on the top of a roof and I just give a wee push off and away I float. I can jump through the air for miles, above all the buildings and people below, floating around for ever . . .'

'Mmmm.'

'And sometimes when I go inside you, for the first time maybe, or when I've been in before but then come out and then I go in again, I feel like I'm walking into a room – aye, that's it – it's all dark, and then I see this door and it's bright inside and I go into the room.'

'What's in the room?'

'Nothing, it's just . . . light, there's light in it. But it's empty, an empty room, full of light, and I go in.'

There was silence for half a minute. His hand stopped moving on her hair. Then she stirred, moving slightly so she was lying on the floor at his side. He leant back on one arm, stretched his legs out, looked down at her. Her eyes were open, red-rimmed, staring at something: the milk and matches on the floor behind him.

'I've just remembered something I was thinking too,' she said. 'Something I was seeing. It was just when you said you saw things, suddenly I remembered. It was last night. Mind how, quite near the end, you were holding me from behind? We were lying on our sides and you had one arm round under my head and down across here.' She placed an arm across her chest. 'And your other arm was over the top and you were rubbing me there as you went in and out. And I remember . . . I was staring at the wall there, it was good, but I was staring at the wall in the dark, and I'm sure my eyes were still open, but I saw something. Somehow I saw something.' She paused, breathing.

'What?' he said after a moment. 'What was it you saw?'

'It was the inside of a shoebox. It was all sort of opened up. I could see right in from the end, it was black inside. It was black outside too, but the edges of the box were there, I saw them. Somehow I knew that's what it was: a shoebox.'

He didn't say anything. He looked across at the wall on her side of the bed.

'What do you think it means?' she said.

'Eh . . .' He lifted her head from his lap. 'Hold on,' he said. 'I'm getting pins and needles.' He swung his legs out from under her and got to his feet, then stepped through the scattered food and away. He crossed to the window and looked out over the roofs and chimneys.

'Well,' she said. 'What does it mean?'

He stared out of the window, unblinking, then slowly leant forward so his forehead was resting on the glass. 'I don't know,' he said at last.

'Don't you?' she said. 'I do.'

Candia McWilliam was born in Edinburgh in 1955. She has three children and has written three novels and one collection of short stories.

How You Look At It

By Candia McWilliam

The getaway was slow, and started late.

Although the weather was fine, there had been a problem with the roll-on roll-off when one vehicle with a trailer wouldn't reverse down cleanly into its place on the car deck. The driver hadn't the knack and got flustered while the CalMac men barked instructions like shepherds to their dogs.

It was as if it was the driver's first time reversing a trailer. If so, why start learning on a crowded car ferry at the height of the season?

Geordie was desperate to get away before they found it. He'd only done it because he'd been desperate and here he was, more desperate so's to get away and never, he now hoped, be seen again, no matter what the shock and misery he'd leave behind him when they found out, each of them.

Would the boat never leave? He sat in his old coat out on deck at the seaward side, trying not to draw attention and hoping that trying didn't its very self draw attention. His knee shook unless he held it down with his drinking hand that was shaking too till he got to the bar. If he could face it.

He'd had to do it.

It would break at least one heart, what he'd done, but how could he not? He could hear everything extra-clear as the time stretched past when the boat should leave, should have left, had not. It was the clearness of nerves and the clearness of talk thrown across water, from the jetty to the folk on the ferry.

If the boat didn't get off soon, someone would find it – it and her – and the game would be up. You couldn't hold talk once it was out.

They'd not know it had been him at once, but he'd hoped to disappear once they arrived at Oban, just hitch down to Glasgow or take a belt over to Inverness, big places where what he had done would make no difference, no one would know and very likely, if they should get to know, no one would care.

He'd had to do it when he'd seen her like that. She'd needed what he'd done. She was asking for it, begging. She was all red in the face like he'd not seen her since they were weans and doing running races down the beach with all sand in their sandshoes and whisking round and round with big woody horses' tails of seaweed till they let them go and they whanged out and you were just grateful there was no one there to get thrummed by them. She was red in the face just before he'd done the thing, like women are; only when. His thought finished the sentence with a picture. It was all red and pink.

Geordie knew it, now, he'd seen it with his wife, just before the when. Red, like to cry, then quiet after a jettering of screams and shakes.

Well, he had known fat Ena that long, and he'd seen her face close up too in the school and when they'd sat quiet to listen when older ones started to come back with stories of the mainland and the stuff to be had over there, long shelves all of the same thing, different types of the same thing, not like the shop out here on the island, where the one can of peaches sat an inchaways from the biros in a jar and the darrows for the fish and a carton of stockings.

Ena was greedy, not just the fat kind of greedy, the inner pull; he'd heard it by her staying silent at the stories of the loaded shelves, she was planning for the day she might take to the sea and begin to spend on the other side of it. She never got off though, not like Geordie. She'd stuck on the island.

It irked him, that staying. She'd got herself a man, a house, a brood, a garden, a wee business and a settled look, as though the fire of the greed was kept well away by deep peats of contentment. He'd not have that. Ena, fat Ena, a cut above.

A cut above. Not that he'd touched her like that.

He was greedy, too, he felt it early on. Nothing was enough for him. He'd liked catalogues, when the post brought them, even as a wean, and he hated for his mother to touch them and read them and make her marks before he got the look in. He took to the pages with domestic items, stiff ladies standing like ballerinas in pinnies saying, 'See how this useful nozzle fulfils every household need and bend me right over', with their flick-up hair and useless fanny fingers.

His greed filled him up, making him hungrier, over the years, till it propelled him off the island towards something he knew he could smell. When Wee Margaret said she'd a vocation to be a nurse one time when they were out the back of the hall having a Tennent's (the can with a girl on, cradling her bosoms like boxer pup heads, she was that old), Geordie kept up the feeling he was doing of her shoulder bone and the salt cellars at her neck, but he thought, 'That's it. I've a vocation too, and it's to get things,' and he felt filled with a glamour. It was like there was nothing you could do about the worst bit of yourself. It was relaxing, like giving in.

At last the ferry was gathering its skirts for the off, water swilling around under, with a froth of white out the edges. He was shaking. The air was colder and a white star arrived modestly in the not much darker sky. He smelt the good smell of the cafeteria, a smell like gravy and curry. There was sweat down his back.

He wanted to add his own force to the screw of the boat that was shoving it away over the water away from the island where he had done what he had done.

He could never go back. A place like the town, you did a thing like this, lost yourself a while and you could still live in the place, enjoy its benefits.

Now he saw he had done a little thing and it was the worst thing he could do.

He had not even made a mistake. He had taken his life and wrung out the good of it with a trivial wee twist because for an instant it had felt right.

Would he tell, when he met up with Fiona again? Would it come out like a relief? The thought was not worth even nodding to. You'd not entertain it.

Fiona was the right one for his greed vocation, the one who saw his worst and assumed it was how we all are really. Fiona had the greed, and she'd fed it and watered it till it was near a virtue. Her greed kept her clean and reliable and a good worker at the shop. It kept her scented nice, it kept their house nice, it sheltered their marriage from getting shook by other men. It just needed filling up, like their nice car.

So. Had Geordie done it, out here on the island, a place Fiona visited only when she couldn't very well not, *for* Fiona? Had he thought Fiona would need what he had taken?

Would it fill her up in the places where she kept her greed? It was certain that it would not.

They were further now from the island and he took a turn, keeping his eyes held in from meeting the eyes of others on the boat, back to the stern of the boat. There was a big whiff of metal and fuel and at the same time a shimmering air that came against his cheeks like off of big wings, lighter than wind. In it was the taste of the sea.

He looked back to the island that seemed to be breathing at him.

It knew him.

Shortly it would know more of him, and would no longer wish to know him. The boat rounded the tip of land that held behind it the beach with whistling sand that rumoured under your feet if you wheeshed them bare along it. Offshore, a narrow soft-bottomed water race from there, lay the small island where he and Margaret had gone first for shells and, later, to touch.

It was no shape, a little eruption of rock mixture dribbled over the island's own shore, but you made it into things with your eyes if you lay there in the sun and slitted your eyes, like looking up close, close at a person when they are bare and could be hills.

The island was shifting in its greater but still small, ever smaller shape too, as they withdrew, all of them, from it in the boat, but he for ever.

In the folds of the land, that were turning their bland evening swell to him before the rocky cuts came into view, lights came out to answer the modest star above.

Over the tannoy came the announcements about the purchase of travel tickets, about the bar and the cafeteria.

People began to move into the lighted parts of the boat. The entrances were all high, so's you'd to lift your feet to get in over them, and the doors were heavy like to keep you out. There were handles stiff with paint and rust on the portholes. It was like a big safe, a safe holding light, with him outside of it, the middle of the ferry.

Still, although he had done what he had done, he was without satisfaction, his greed stinging him as he looked into the warm, into the families, as he imagined, taking their chips, the men going in groups to the bar for whiskies and bringing cans out up to the wives.

There was a black and white collie bitch out on the deck, her leash tied through the slats and coir rope of one of those varnished old benches that are meant to double as life-rafts.

For a moment, Geordie took it into his head to talk to the dog, but soon enough he could tell it did not want to talk to him. He saw by the look in its eye that he was known.

The island was sending out its last revelation of itself to him, powdery falls of grey and blue land cracking across its fault – its *fault*, its geological fault – into shiny brittle rock startled with the last, roosting white birds, and the crowning sickle of the whitest beach, and he contemplated what he had done, taken money he did not need and a woman he did not want, and had never wanted simply to make his one home tell him what he was evidently greedy to proclaim about himself, that he was no longer at home anywhere.

At last, he realised, planning his destination, he had nowhere to be at rest. He settled to sleep on the life-raft bench and the sleep when it came was no thicker than grease on water.

Denise Mina worked as an auxiliary nurse in a geriatric and terminal care nursing home before returning to education and studying law at Glasgow University. While studying for a PhD on the gendered application of legal psychiatry she wrote Garnethill, *which won the Creasey Memorial Dagger for Best First Novel 1998.* Garnethill *is the first in a trilogy of crime novels and is currently being adapted for television.*

Carol's Gift

By Denise Mina

It was one of those amazing times when things seem like they were meant. I saw the signs and read them. I was looking for a future, for signs, because my mind was confused. They'd made me say bad things about Carol. My three months in the village was the first time since her that I'd been alone with my thoughts, allowed to pore over the memory of her, the texture of her voice. The first amazing thing happened three days after I came to stay in the village; there had been a big storm the night before and the next day the sea started spewing up fire. We watched it through the loading bay doors at lunch time. Bubbles of orange and blue fire burst on the surface of the jaggy, grey sea. They were incredibly beautiful. The odds against it happening just as I came, just as I was looking for signs, were so long it had to mean something. I watched them and knew they were there for me. The guys at work even commented on it. 'You've brought them with ye, Tam.' I smiled, giving them what they expected. I wanted their attention away from me. I don't like being watched, being seen. I'm not mental, just private.

They explained the fires on the radio; sixty years before, a Nazi submarine was in trouble and started dipping just outside the harbour. The crew panicked and dumped a load of fire bombs, afraid they'd go off on board if they hit the bottom. The bombs were heavy, they were wrapped in cast iron jackets, and they tumbled down a hill under the water, tumbling into a deep, dark valley. They nestled in the valley, miles under the sea. Then I arrived and big Summer storms blew out of nothing just as the cast iron was rotten enough to snap and let go. The undertow sucked the bombs out of their casings and along the dark valley, setting them free. The bombs flew to the surface, like bubbles in ginger, hissing damp, tired old flames over the surface, and then they died, fulfilled at last. They'd waited under the water for fifty years, keeping quiet, waiting for their time to come. I know what it takes to do that. The bombs meant that my time was coming. I would pass my test. I would drive through the Summer valley.

No one in the village liked the bombs except for me. The fishermen said they were a pain in the arse, they had to watch out for the fires on the surface and steer around them. The village was losing money as well because the tourists only came for day trips that year. They watched the bombs burst for a while but then left and drove down the coast to the prettier towns and spent their money there. An MOD unit went down to see how many bombs were left and one of the men got his breathing stuff caught on a rock. He was dead when they brought him to the surface.

I was working in the soap factory, loading boxes into the vans. The big wooden doors looked out to sea and every time there had been a storm the workers gathered around the door, eating their lunch, watching the bombs and complaining about them. They came back every time there was a storm, knowing the bombs would be there, missing their lunch hour to watch them and moan. I didn't join in, I kept to myself, but my heart swelled whenever I heard them phut and sizzle or saw the flashes of brilliant light defying the grey consensus. Every bomb was a reminder that my time was coming, that soon I would pass my test and buy my van. I'd drive my van through the Summer valley with my hand resting on the wheel, warmed by the sun.

I go on about driving the van, I know I do, but it means so much to me. I only got to drive my van for a few days but I still dream about it, even after what happened, even when the other meaning is so clear. I'll tell ye the dream. I'm driving a small van through a valley in the country, by a river; sometimes I'm listening to the radio, sometimes I'm not. My arm is straight out in front of me holding the wheel, loose like, as if I've had a long drive and my arms are tired. It's a small van but there's a cabin behind me, a private space so that I can lie down if I need to, if it gets dark. I know I won't need to stop anywhere or see anyone and I can move on whenever I need to. The first time I had the dream was about . . . six years? . . . six odd years into the last sentence, the long one I got for taking Carol's gift. I love it. I feel happy for hours when I've had that dream. I could lie about it, I can tell ye I'm sorry I dream it, that it makes me sick, but they can't add time on to forever so what's the point? I love my dream.

At the soap factory someone told the foreman I was taking driving lessons. He came up to me in front of the other men in the loading bay and told me he would never give me a driving job because I'd been in prison. He stared at me and sucked his teeth and then he walked away. He meant to shame me but he didn't. I turned away and smiled to myself, not letting the others see. He didn't know what I'd been in for, if he knew he'd've said it, he was that kind of man. And best of all, if he didn't know what I'd been in for, then no one else knew either, Constable Hay didn't tell them. Hay's eyes were heavy and sad when he saw me. He knew my Gran and I suppose he shut up for her sake. I didn't care as long as he kept it to hisself.

I was allowed to move to the village because my people were from there. My mother moved away when she heard I was coming and Gran died soon after I arrived. They offered me her house but it was too big and had a garden. I couldn't manage a big place. I'd been inside too long. They got me a single room in Mr MacCallum's house.

They got me the job in the soap factory. It was a good job except for the smell of soap; it was terrible. It got up my nose and settled at the bridge, making my eyes water. When I blew my nose at the end of a day the hankie would be full of stinking silver stuff. Everyone who worked there smelled of soap but the ones who worked the factory floor smelt the worst. If I touched the walls in the factory or sat down anywhere the smell stuck to me. On windy days the smell covered the town and only the rain could deaden it.

I made £120 a week at the job. Mr MacCallum got thirty quid, ten went on smoke, fifteen on food, thirty on driving lessons (two a week) and the rest of it went into the bank, where it stayed until the day I bought my van.

Because Hay kept his mouth shut the people at the factory didn't know anything about me. I was a big city mystery, a country boy gone to live in Glasgow with his father when he was eleven, and they knew my mother's people. It was a good few weeks before I was spotted going to sign my slip at Hay's house. When the guys at work asked me about it I told them I'd been done for armed robbery. They believed me. They treated me better afterwards, treated me with respect, and some of the women tried to talk to me. One lunch time the foreman gave me a fag. He said to come to the pub after work with the rest of them. I said mibbie but I didn't go. I'm private.

Just after that the wages guy took me aside during a fag break. He told me about Diane and her family. He said that she was a widow and she fancied me, I should ask her out. That lunch time I saw her looking at me. The others were crowded around the bay doors watching the bombs go off and I looked up and saw her watching me slyly, keeping her face seawards, sliding her red, excited eyes towards me. I didn't know what to do. It was a long time since I'd spoken to a woman and I was shy of them. I still am shy of them. It doesn't matter now, I don't think I'll ever meet another one.

It was only a week until my final driving test and I already had a hundred quid on a secondhand van in Grath's. I wanted to asked Diane to go out with me; she had a job and she didn't go with a lot of men so she wasn't a slag or anything. I could've asked her out to the pub but then we would have to talk to each other. I didn't know what to do until one night when I was walking home from work. I leaned on the harbour wall and looked up. I looked at that exact spot at exactly the right time and I saw two bombs arrive at the surface at exactly the same time. They bobbed on the sea for a breath's length and then exploded at the same time, their flames touching. It was dark and the coloured flames were amazing against the water; they took my breath away, they were so close. I stayed by the wall, watching until they died, and when I lit a fag my hands were shaking. And that was another sign. I knew it would be alright with Diane.

The day after I saw the two bombs Diane came over to me and asked me to go to the pictures with her. I managed to say 'aye' and she smiled at me, making me blush more, and walked away. The bombs were right. It was okay. I was reading the signs right this time and that got me thinking, maybe I'd always been reading the signs right.

I was looking forward to going out with Diane and a night at the pictures was perfect because we wouldn't need to speak much. I was still thinking about Carol. I couldn't decide what I thought about it, my mind was still messed up by the stuff they'd told us in the group. But the signs proved themselves true this time; it was a confusing time.

I didn't think I'd miss that group but I did. The other guys said I was lucky to be getting out, to get away from the group helpers, and I thought so too but I missed the men, missed being with them and talking to them. We had our own special group in that prison, we had our own special everything because we couldn't mix with the other prisoners. They called us filth and attacked us. They threatened to kill us and they meant it too, they killed one of our old guys. He was in the showers and some guys stabbed him. They announced it in group and told us to be more careful. I felt sad about it, which was funny because I didn't know him much. I know the others were sad too, even if they didn't say it. It was as if we had all died a bit. I kept his glasses, to remember him. I don't think anyone else will remember him, he never had a letter or visitors. The other prisoners hated us but I couldn't see how we were different. We all took things we shouldn't have.

No one gives a shit about us, not the wives that wait or the relatives that visit and pretend it was all lies or the helpers at the group. My own Mum doesn't visit me or send me food or write me letters or phone me. She came to see me once after Carol and it was all *heartbreak, shame* and *godforgive wicked evil man that child that child*. I can understand why she said it now, since the group, but I'm her own son for God's sake. If she was going to pick sides I think it should have been mine. I suppose she's read the papers and knows what happened this time. I'd refuse to see her if she came now.

I missed that group. Sometimes I would lie in bed at Mr MacCallum's and think about the guys in the group. I liked it best when the others talked, not me. I'm private but that wasn't allowed. They asked me about Carol, making me tell them what happened over and over, asking how she died. The questions were stupid, we all worked out that we had to tell the story a special way or we'd be in trouble. I've seen stupid men telling the story the wrong way. The helpers went for them, said they were in denial and asked more horrible questions. We all hated the helpers. They weren't bad people, they just didn't understand about us. We understood each other in ways they couldn't fathom. I remember Jamie telling a story in the wrong way. He wasn't stupid, he did it for badness. He wanted to wind them up and it worked as well. It was a story about creeping through the house at night, about hands on skin, about smells from hair. He could make you feel as if you were there. Ages before the helpers realised and stopped him the rest of us were grinning at each other and laughing. We knew how he was telling the story. We knew. Jamie wouldn't lie to please them.

I listened to the things they said in group. I didn't like it, it made me uncomfortable, especially at first. It was all about denial and admitting the damage you had done and changing your behaviour, changing your thinking. They made me talk about Carol and telling them made me lie about what had happened between us. I had to tell our story the way they wanted to hear it or lose remission. But Carol, my Carol, I was betraying her, I told lies about her and about myself and about what happened. As I denounced myself I was denouncing Carol's gift because I read her signs, the looks from her and her touch, the clothes she wore and the truth was that I didn't take her life, Carol gave it to me.

I stopped lying to myself about Carol the night I went to the pictures with Diane. We went to see a film about a pig and she invited me back to her house. I was nervous because my driving test was in a couple of days and Diane smelled of soap so much it made me sneeze. Nothing happened between us, which was good. She cooked us some oven chips. She had three sons and a daughter called Morag and Morag was my next sign.

At work Diane came over to talk to me, to wish me good luck because my driving test was in the afternoon. Some of the other women were watching and giggling. She was very flirty, trying to be sexy with me. She wasn't like that when we were alone and I preferred it when she wasn't. She touched my hand and the smell of soap stuck to me. I couldn't eat my sandwiches because of her smell.

I sat my driving test. I passed it. First time. I went home to Mr MacCallum's and sat on the end of the bed. If I'd believed in God I would have given thanks but I don't. The feelings built up inside me, growing and growing until I thought I would burst. Outside of the window a storm was brewing, a thick dark storm, the worst storm of the whole Summer, and the rain smashed against the wee window in my room. I couldn't believe it. I remember I sat on my bed and smoked a fag to stop myself from crying. My dream was coming true, the signs were everywhere, I could drive anywhere. Outside, the storm windows were slamming shut on the houses all over the village. I couldn't hold it in any more. I crept out of the house through the back door and climbed up to the hills overlooking the sea. I climbed further than walking distance, up to where I was scrabbling on scree; I wanted to get as high up as possible.

When I finally stopped and sat down the rain was thinner and I felt very warm from the effort. I took off my coat to cool down. I rolled a cigarette and by the time I lit it I was smiling because I knew what I was really there for. I was out of denial now.

I looked out to sea and saw the bombs going off; there were so many, the water was covered with fire of all colours, far off into the horizon, like a million Viking funerals. My time had come. I undid my fly and slipped my hand inside. And then I wasn't sitting on the side of the rainy hill, I was driving my red van from Grath's, driving through a valley in the Summer with my private space in the back. My arm was tired because I'd been driving for a while and maybe I was smoking I don't know. I could feel the warm sun on my arm and next to me on the seat was little Morag, not yet crying, not yet afraid, and the smell of soap was far far behind us both.

Agnes Owens was born in 1926 and lives in Scotland. She is the author of Gentlemen of the West, Lean Tales *(with James Kelman and Alasdair Gray)*, Like Birds in the Wilderness, A Working Mother, People Like That *and* For the Love of Willie.

A Change of Face

By Agnes Owens

I was five pounds short of the two hundred I needed by Thursday, and I had only two days to make it up.

'Why do you need two hundred pounds?' asked Ingrid, my room-mate.

'Let's say I promised myself that amount.'

'That explains everything,' she said. 'I once promised myself a holiday in Majorca, but things don't always work out.'

'In your case things never work out.'

'I think you're crazy,' said Ingrid. 'What good is money to you anyway?' Her fatuity was maddening but I kept calm.

'Lend me a fiver. You won't regret it.'

Her tinny laugh pierced my ear. 'What me? With scarcely a bean!'

'Get out,' I said, 'before I cripple you.'

She folded down her tartan skirt and walked out the door with a hoity-toity air, ludicrous, I thought, in a down-and-out whore. I waited a good five minutes to make sure she was gone before I fetched the briefcase from under my bed. I never failed to be impressed by the look of it. Good-quality leather was more in my line than the trash Ingrid flaunted. The briefcase had originally belonged to one of her clients. I remembered his piggish stamp of respectability. Mind you, that was ten years before when Ingrid was in better condition. He had left it by the side of the bed, complete with lock and key and containing two stale sandwiches, while Ingrid slept off her labours. I explained later I had found it in a dustbin. Once again I counted the money acquired in pounds and pence but it still totalled only one hundred and ninety-five.

In Joe's Eats Café I leaned over the counter. 'Joe,' I asked, 'how's about lending me a couple of quid? Five to be exact. Until the Giro comes on Saturday.'

Joe kept his eyes on the trickle of heavy tea he was pouring. He breathed hard. 'What for?'

'Oh, I don't know. Who needs money?'

'It don't pay to lend money. I should know.'

'Of course, never a borrower or a lender be,' I said, fishing for ten pence.

'I've been done before. No reflection on you.'

I looked round, then leaned over and whispered. 'You can have a free shot and I'll still owe you the fiver.'

He recoiled then hooted with laughter. 'You must be joking – not even with a bag over your head.'

I shrugged and put on what passed for a smile. 'It's your loss. I know some new tricks.'

Joe patted my shoulder. 'I know you mean well, Lolly, but you're not my taste – nothing personal.'

We brooded together for a bit. Finally Joe said, 'Ingrid might lend it to you.'

'Not her.'

'Oh well.' He turned to pour water into the pot.

'I've got one hundred and ninety-five pounds.' I threw at him. His back stiffened.

'What's the problem then?'

I knew I was wasting my time but I explained. 'I need two hundred by Thursday. It would alter my whole life.'

He chortled. 'You paying for a face lift or something?'

'Better than that.'

He shook his head. 'Sorry kid, you see—'

I took my cup of tea over to the table without listening. Ten minutes later I was strolling along a quiet part of the city occupied mainly by decaying mansions.

'I'm short of a fiver,' I explained to the tall man in the black suit.

His eyes glowed with regret. 'I'm sorry. Two hundred is the price. I can't accept less.'

'Will it be too late after Thursday?'

'I'm afraid so.' He could not have been more sympathetic.

'What should I do – steal?'

'I can give you no advice.'

He closed the door gently in my face and left me staring at the peeling paint. A cat leapt on to the step and wound itself round my legs. I picked it up and forced it to look at my face. 'Stupid animal,' I said, as it purred its pleasure. I threw it away from me and returned home.

I walked into the bedroom and grabbed Ingrid by her sparse hair as she lay splayed over Jimmy Font, identifiable by his dirty boots.

'Out,' I shouted.

She pulled on her grey vest screaming. 'I'll kill you.'

Jimmy thrashed about like a tortoise on its back clutching his privates as if they were gold.

I towered above him. 'Hurry!' He gained his feet, made the sign of the cross, grabbed his trousers and ran.

'May you burn in hell,' moaned Ingrid, rubbing a bald patch on her head.

I tossed over a handful of hair. 'Before you go, take that filth with you.'

'Where can I go?' she sobbed.

'The gutter, the river, the madhouse. Take your choice.'

She pulled on her dress. 'I don't feel well.' I didn't answer. 'Anyway,' she added, 'if you had let Jimmy stay I might have earned a fiver to lend you.'

I was not swayed by her logic. A drink from Jimmy's bottle would have been the price. I walked out of the room to escape from her staleness.

At one time they had told me in the hospital plastic surgery could eventually work wonders. I did not like the word 'eventually'. Civilly I had requested that they terminate my breath, but they merely pointed out how lucky I was to be given the opportunity. Suspecting they would only transform me into a different kind of monster I had left them studying diagrams. That happened a long time ago, but I still had my dreams of strolling along an avenue of trees holding up a perfect profile to the sun.

'Are you listening?' said Ingrid, breaking through my thoughts with some outrageous arrangement she would fix for me to get five pounds. She backed away when I headed towards her. As she ran through the door and down the stairs I threw out her flea-ridden fur coat, which landed on her shoulders like the mottled skin of a hyena.

The Salvation Army Band on the street corner blared out its brassy music of hope. I settled down on the bench beside Teddy the tramp and spun thoughts of fine wire in my head.

'Nice?' commented Teddy from the depths of an abandoned army coat. He offered me a pale-green sandwich from a bread paper, which I declined.

'We have much to be thankful for,' he said, as he bit into the piece.

A body of people gathered on the far side. The music stopped. Everyone applauded. I joined the group, who courteously stood their ground when I brushed close. My eyes were on the Sally Ann coming towards us with trusting goodwill and the collection box in her hand. I slipped my hand beneath the other hands holding out donations, then tugged the string loosely held by the good lady, and ran.

Six pounds and forty-seven pence lay strewn over my bed in pence and silver. I blessed the kindness of the common people and the compassion of the Salvation Army, who would never persecute or prosecute a sorry person like me. Tomorrow was Thursday and I had the two hundred pounds, with one pound forty-seven to the good. With a mixture of joy and fear I poured five pounds into the briefcase. Then I studied a single sheet of parchment, the words on which I knew by heart. The message was direct and unfanciful, and unaccountably I believed it, perhaps because of its simplicity, and also the power which emanated from the black hand-writing. Even the mercenary demand for two hundred pounds strength-ened my belief in a force much deeper than plastic surgery. I calculated there must always be a price to pay, which for effort's sake should go beyond one's means, to accomplish results.

All evening Ingrid did not return. I wasn't surprised or sorry. In my mind's eye I could see her tossing against dank alley walls in drunken confusion – her wispy hair falling like damp thistledown over her forehead, her eyes rolling around like those of an old mare about to be serviced. Not that I wished her to be any different. Her degradation had afforded me stature, though after tomorrow I hoped never to see her again. Fancying a bout of self-torture to pass the time, I began searching for a mirror, suspecting it would be useless since I had forbidden them in the flat. I peered at my reflection in the window. Like a creature from outer space it stared back without pity. Satisfactorily sickened I raised two fingers, then turned away.

'See your pal Ingrid,' declared Maidy Storr, when I passed her stall of old hats, shoes and rusty brooches.

'Not recently.'

'She stole a bundle of money from Dan Riley when he dozed off in Maitland's bar last night.'

'Never.'

'Well, she did. I sat on one side of him and she was on the other. I remember she left quickly without finishing her drink. Next thing he woke up shouting he'd been robbed.'

'How much' I asked.

'Fifty quid, he said. Mind you I was surprised he had that much.' She added winking, 'You'll be all right for a tap.'

'Haven't seen her since yesterday morning.'

'Done a bunk, has she?'

'Couldn't say.'

'Well, she would, wouldn't she? The law will be out for her.'

'For stealing from a pickpocket? I don't see Dan complaining.'

Maidy frowned. 'I see what you mean. It makes you sick to think she'll get away with it.'

'Couldn't care less whether she gets away with it or not.' I picked up a single earring. 'Have you many one-eared customers?'

'Leave that stuff and get going.'

I walked away quickly when Maidy threw a shoe at me, and headed towards Joe's for breakfast.

'I think I'd like something special today,' I informed him.

'How about some weedkiller?' he suggested.

'I said something special, not the usual.' I considered his confined choices.

'Be quick and move to your seat before the joint gets busy.' Being a liberal-minded fellow Joe allowed me in his place when it was quiet, provided I sat in the alcove behind the huge spider plant. I chose a pizza and a glass of tomato juice.

'Living it up,' he sneered.

'Might as well. Anyway, I'm tired of the little creatures in your meat pies.'

I could see Joe looking anxiously at a neatly dressed old lady approaching. Hastily I moved to the alcove with my pizza and tomato juice. The old lady was having an intense conversation with Joe. I suspected she was complaining about me. I finished my pizza and deliberately took my tomato juice over to a centre table. At a table nearby a couple with a child looked at me, aghast. The child wailed. I smiled at them, or in my case, grimaced. The child's wails increased in volume. Joe charged over and signalled for me to get out. The neat old lady appeared out of the steam.

'Don't you know this is a friend of mine?' she said, looking hard at Joe then bestowing a loving smile on me. Joe looked unconvinced, but he was stumped.

'If you say so.' He moved the couple and the child behind the spider plant.

The old lady sat down beside me and said, 'I'm sorry you have to put up with this sort of thing.'

I shrugged. 'That's all right.'

'Such a lack of kindness is terrible,' she continued.

'I suppose so.'

'Can I get you something?' she asked.

'A pizza, if you don't mind.'

She attended to me smartly. I could feel her eyes boring through me as I ate. She cleared her throat and asked, 'Are you often exposed to such er – abuse?'

'Don't worry about it,' I said. 'You'll only upset yourself.' Her eyes were brimming over by this time and I couldn't concentrate on eating.

'Is there nothing that can be done?' she asked just as I had the fork half-way up to my mouth.

'About what?' I was really fed up with her. I find it impossible to talk and eat at the same time.

'I mean, my dear – what about plastic surgery – or something?'

I threw down my fork. 'Listen, if you don't like the way I look, bugger off.' I paid her no further attention when she left.

'That's another customer you've lost me,' Joe called over. I told him to bugger off too, then hastily departed.

For the remainder of the day I kept checking on the time, which meant I had to keep searching for the odd clock in shop windows. I half-expected to bump into Ingrid. In a way I would have been glad to see her, because even if she was completely uninteresting, in her vapid manner she used to converse with me. She was still out when I returned home, no doubt holed up somewhere, frightened to stir in case she met Riley. I washed my face, combed my hair, put on a fresh jumper and looked no better than before, but at least it was a gesture. Then I checked the money in the briefcase and left without a backward glance. I headed slowly to my destination so that I would arrive on the exact minute of the hour of my appointment. Normally I don't get excited easily, for seldom is there anything to get excited about, but I must admit my heart was pounding when I stood on the steps of the shabby mansion. The tall man in the black suit received my briefcase solemnly. He bowed, then beckoned me to follow him.

'Are you not going to count the money?' I asked.

His sepulchral voice resounded down the corridor. 'If you have faith in me I know the money will be correct.'

I wanted to ask questions but I could scarcely keep pace as he passed smoothly ahead of me. Abruptly he stopped outside a door and turned. The questions died on my lips as I met his opaque glance. It was too late to have doubts so I allowed him to usher me into the room. I can give no explanation for what followed because once inside I was dazzled by a translucent orange glow so powerful that all my senses ceased to function. I knew nothing until I woke up outside the corridor holding on to the tall man. Even in that state of mesmerism I knew I was different. My lips felt rubbery and my eyes larger. Tears were running down my cheeks, which in itself was a strange thing, since I had not cried for years. The man carefully escorted me into another room and placed me before a mirror, saying, 'Don't be afraid. You will be pleased.'

I breathed deep, and looked. I didn't say anything for a time because the image that faced me was that of Ingrid. I leaned forward to touch her, but it was only the glass of a mirror.

'You are much nicer now?' the man asked in an ingratiating manner.

What could I say? I didn't want to complain, but I had been definitely altered to be the double of Ingrid. Certainly the face was the same, and we had been of similar build anyway.

'Very nice,' I croaked. 'Thank you very much.'

His lips curled into what could have been a smile, then he tapped me on the shoulder to get going. I shook hands with him when I stood on the step outside, clutching my empty briefcase.

'It's a funny thing –' I began to say, but he had vanished behind the closed door.

It might have been a coincidence but Ingrid never showed up. This was convenient because everyone assumed I was Ingrid, so I settled into her way of life and discovered it wasn't too bad. Certainly it has its ups and downs but I get a lot of laughs with her clients and it doesn't hurt my face either. The only snag is, now and again I worry about bumping into Dan Riley. Sometimes I consider saving up for a different face, but that might be tempting fate. Who knows what face I would get? Besides, I have acquired a taste for the good things in life, like cigarettes and vodka. So I take my chances and confront the world professionally equipped in a fur jacket and high black boots, trailing my boa feathers behind me.

Siân Preece was born in Wales in 1965. She currently lives in Aberdeen, where she is working on a short story collection, From the Life, *for Polygon. Her work has been broadcast on radio and has appeared in several magazines. She was the recipient of a Scottish Arts Council Writer's Bursary in 1998.*

Second Hand

By Siân Preece

'Rhona, I'm cold. I want to get down.'

But Rhona grasps Melanie's goosy shoulders and holds her there. Body heat slides between them like a slip of paper. In the draught from the window, the waist-high net curtain dances a hula on their thighs.

'He hasn't seen us yet,' says Rhona firmly.

Melanie hears the house creeping up on them; doors whisper on their hinges, the staircarpet concertinas up on itself, ready to explode into the bedroom and catch them. But Rhona seems oblivious.

In the garden next door Mr Lewis bends, slow as a branch, and digs his fingers into the earth. The udder of his brown trousers droops and swings between his legs. There is nothing to do in the garden in December; he has come to get away from Mrs Lewis.

'Turn around!' whispers Rhona, as if he can hear her. Melanie wills him to stay there forever, to root his clodded boots in the soil and grow like a tree; but then he straightens and turns, almost as if they had called him, and looks up. Now they can leap, falling back from the window and tumbling on the carpet, giggling and ticklish.

'Excellent! Oh, excellent!' shrieks Rhona, kicking wildly. 'The timing was perfect! He'll never know if he saw us or not!' It is part of her plan to drive Mr Lewis mad.

'He'd better not. My mother would have my guts for garters.'

'He won't – he'll never be sure. We should have written "hello" on our chests! We should've written "hello" on mine and "Mr Lewis" on yours.' She looks at Melanie. 'See? It was good, wasn't it?'

Melanie shakes her head and smiles. She crawls over to the window, burning her knees on the gritty carpet, and peeps through the curtains.

'He's just standing and looking around. I know! Let's get dressed really quickly and run round by the lane, and stroll past like we're coming back from somewhere.'

'Yeah!'

But neither of them wants to move. The bedroom is cosy and the house has changed its mind about ambushing them. It is enough for them to sit naked together and pretend it's normal. Melanie shuffles, reading the carpet's braille with her bottom, and rubs a cool glass dolphin along her leg.

Rhona's house is a lawless place. You can touch anything, play with anything, stack things by size or by colour, or by how much you like them. The rooms migrate into each other, so there is a lawnmower in the bathroom and books in the beds and Rhona's father in the kitchen. But even Melanie has to admit that it's a mess. You can put a cup of tea down and not find it again for weeks. Each junk-shop armchair is different, and the cats are allowed to pick and scrabble at them as if there are diamonds hidden in the upholstery. In the dining room, a big picture of Jesus has leaned against the wall for two years, waiting to be nailed up.

Rhona herself wears Enid Blyton clothes: print dresses that skim her ankle socks, and a school blazer for a coat. In sewing class, the teacher is always happening to find lengths of spare cloth in the needlework cupboard, and she helps Rhona to make skirts and blouses; but when Melanie comes up with the teacloth that she has been stitching all term, Miss Downie just says: 'Unpick it and start again,' then, 'Well I never, Rhona! Here's a zip that might just fit.'

Melanie stages a fight between two Victorian dolls, and asks casually:
    'Rhona – are you poor?'
    Rhona looks up from drawing on her feet. 'No.' She draws a question mark on her big toe. 'Why?'
    'Dunno. Just wondered.'
    After a pause, Rhona says, 'My father's going to buy a car.'
    'Yeah?'
    'Yeah, he's going to teach me to drive it.'
    'You can't drive, you're too young.' Melanie is angry with the lie. Rhona *said* she wasn't poor; she doesn't have to make things up to impress.
    'You can drive on private land. My father knows a farmer who'll let us.'
    'You can drive in Mr Lewis's garden, then. That'll definitely push him over the edge.'
    Melanie referees while Victoria holds Felicity in a half-nelson for a count of one-two-three-break! The dolls get up and shake hands. 'I went on a tractor once,' she says, unconvincingly. Rhona rolls her eyes.
    'That's living alright!'
    Melanie looks at her wristwatch, the only thing she kept on.
    'I have to go.'
    She pulls on her jeans with the pants still inside and imagines being Rhona. Dressing here each morning among the seashells and kites and ex-army sleeping bags. Having a mother who knocks gently on bedroom doors instead of screaming up the stairs about eggs being like bullets. Then she reaches under the bed for her trainers and finds a dust bunny the size of a netball and one of the cats sucking her shoelace.
    'I'm off,' she says.
    'Thought I could smell something funny!' flashes back Rhona.
    Running home, Melanie wonders if Rhona knows there's a smell to her house, and if her own house would smell as strange if she wasn't used to it.

*   *   *

'She's had that coat.'

Melanie's house smells of fish fingers and mint, and it sounds of television. Her mother is unwrapping After Eights and trying to remember how the posh girl eats them in the pre-Christmas adverts.

'That's the last you'll see of that!' she adds, nibbling daintily at the chocolate corners.

Melanie can't find her coat. Her mother won't let up about it, seems pleased to have something to moan about, something bad to associate with Rhona. Melanie's father sits motionless in his chair, in the belief that this will render him invisible.

'I'll get it tomorrow,' mumbles Melanie.

'Oho, you think you're going there tomorrow, do you?'

'I have to, to get my coat.'

'Don't be clever; your father can go and get it.' Melanie and her father shout 'No!' in unison. 'You should be staying in and concentrating on your school work. Rhona's mother doesn't want *you* hanging around all the time.'

Rhona's mother hardly ever knows they're there. If she wanders into the dining room to find them making a tent or putting on a play, she says, 'Oh! Hello girruls!' and looks at Rhona as if she knows her from somewhere but can't remember her name.

'She doesn't mind,' says Melanie.

'*I* mind! Why can't you play with someone nice like Jane Alexander? You two were friends before that bloody girl came along.'

'Jane Alexander is a snob!'

'Jane Alexander's father is a solicitor! And her mother is a Brown Owl!'

Melanie bites her lip to drive out the image of Mrs Alexander, feathered and bespectacled, tearing at a mouse.

'Don't you laugh, smarty pants! Why don't you join the Brownies?'

'You said I should concentrate on my school work.'

'Don't be clever. Brownies would go on your report.'

'Brownies is Hobbies and Interests,' says Melanie's father.

'Responsibility, John! Brownies is Responsibility.'

Melanie thinks of the vivisection laboratory that she and Rhona made out of cardboard boxes the week before. The cats wouldn't stay put, so they filled it with soft toys. Then they stormed the lab and liberated them, wearing handkerchief masks and shouting 'Freedom for animals!'

'I've got hobbies and interests,' she says.

'Well, God knows what they are! What'll you put on your report? Hanging out with hippies and low-lifes and . . .'

'Gyppos.'

'Tinkers, John! They're tinkers.'

The phone rings and Melanie runs to answer it, knowing it will be Rhona. She's in a call box.

'I'm in a call box!'

'You don't have to shout.'

'What? Look, I've only got one coin. I'll think of a shape in ten minutes, and you think hard and see if you can guess what it is! Okay?'

'Wait! Did I leave my coat with you?'

'Eh? Your coat? No, I haven't seen it. Now, think of that shape in ten minutes and write it down. We'll compare them tomorrow. Bye! There go the . . .'

Melanie drags back to the living room. 'Rhona.'

'As if you haven't just spent all day with her. What did she want?'

Melanie hesitates. She can't mention the telepathy experiment. 'Oh, just to say she hasn't got my coat.' But her mother pounces.

'Knew about that, did she? I told you, she's stolen it. Or else it's lost in that shady, shanty . . .'

'Shithouse.'

'Shed, John! It's a shed, that's what it is . . . Melanie, where are you sloping off to?'

'Shi – toilet.'

Melanie sits on the toilet with a notebook and pencil, and concentrates. Then she lets her mind run free, receptive, but still no shape comes, or none that seems more likely than any other. Eventually she draws the shape of a coat, adding a round hood so that, if Rhona thought of a circle, she can say that's it. For extra insurance, she adds triangular collars and square pockets.

'A shield?' says Melanie the next day. 'Who ever thinks of a shield? What chance did that give me?'

'Why, what did you draw?' says Rhona. Her face falls. 'Oh. Are you still missing your coat?'

'Yeah.'

Rhona folds the paper again and again, creasing the edges with her nails. 'You can only ever do it seven times, even if you start with a piece the size of Wales. Mel. Mel, I didn't take your coat. I'm your best friend, Mel.'

'Yeah.'

'Melly. Smelly Melly. Come on . . . hey, do you want to see a secret?'

'It's not them fairies again, is it?'

'No, it's not fairies!'

'Cause we waited an hour . . .'

'Shut up! I was a kid then!'

It had been five months ago, sitting by the river while Rhona sang softly to attract the wee folk, and the mud soaked Melanie's shorts right through to the knickers.

'I got a hell of a row for my shorts.'

'Look; d'you want to see it or not?'

'What is it?'

'My father's Christmas present.' Wheedling, 'It's in the attic.'

'Alright then. But quickly; I'm only supposed to have come for my coat.'

Melanie's father had recently been into their attic for the Christmas decorations. His feet dangled through the hole as he swore and dropped the torch, and his slippers doodlebugged one by one on to the landing. Afterwards, he banged the hatch shut and double-locked it as if the first Mrs Rochester were up there.

Rhona's attic is so completely integrated into the house that it has a sweet little ladder of its own that clangs as they climb it. At the top, they are welcomed by a tailor's dummy in a shroud, with a television ariel sticking from its neck like a surprised head.

'That's it.' says Rhona.

'What – the dummy?'

'No, stupid! The dummy's *wearing* it. It's a suit.'

Melanie walks a wary circle round the suit, expecting mouse heads to pop from the pockets and cuffs. Close up, it has a cabbage smell.

'So. Rhona. This suit . . . is knitted. It's a knitted suit, Rhona!'

'My mother made it!' says Rhona proudly. 'It's natural dyes and everything – that's why it's green.'

'Rhona! I mean – your Dad's got to weigh twenty-five stone! He's going to look like the Quatermass experiment!'

'Oh, r-really?' says Rhona, sounding like her mother. 'And what's your father getting?'

'Socks and soaps and slippers and a packet of Whiffs to smoke on Boxing Day. In the shed. Outside if fine.' Melanie's father always laughs when he says that but she doesn't know why.

'Well, I think it's boring.'

'Well, I think it's normal!'

Melanie turns away and mooches among the trunks and boxes. 'Any more secrets up here?'

'Well, there's *my* presents,' says Rhona shyly.

'You know your Christmas presents?'

'Don't you?'

'Some of them. Stuff I asked for. But I'm getting surprises too; I'm getting a Haunted House and Slime.'

'Oh, right; *surprises!*'

'I looked in the wardrobe. Why, what are you getting?'

Rhona draws a circle in the dust with her toe. 'Don't tell.'

'What?'

'Don't *tell!*'

'Alright, alright! What?'

'A bike.' Rhona tilts her chin. 'See? We're not poor.'

Melanie stares, then punches the air. 'Great! A bike! That's brilliant, we can go on our bikes together now!' She usually has to give Rhona a backie, and Rhona's skirts get caught in the chain and look like they've been chewed by an oily shark. 'So, where is it?'

Melanie casts around the attic for the spoky shapes and proportions that seem so familiar until you try to draw them; she tried for weeks in anticipation of her own birthday bike. 'Is that it? Under the curtain?' She draws it back in a velvety, stagy ripple. 'Yes, it – oh, wow, Rhona! It's a Chopper!'

'I know.' Rhona starts hopping around, nervous. 'Leave it now, Mel.'

'But Rhona, a Chopper is mega! You'll be like Ruth Williams, she's got a Chopper. Well, she did. She had a new one, and it wasn't even for Christmas; my mother says they must have a money tree in the garden.'

'Yeah,' says Rhona miserably. 'Leave it, Mel.'

'And it's red too! Ruth's was yellow, but red's best – and look, here's a bell to go on it, but it'll have to go on the side, because with Choppers . . . Oh.'

Melanie stops just as Rhona shouts: 'Mel! I said *leave it*!'

The bell clatters and pings on the wooden beams.

'Rhona . . .' says Melanie, very carefully 'Rhona, this is Ruth's bike.'

Rhona stares at her. 'It is *not*!'

It becomes very quiet in the attic. Melanie gets a faint buzz in her ears, as if she can hear the dust settling around them. Squinting at the bike, she sees the light red spray where paint has spattered on the chrome.

'Someone's resprayed this bike! Rhona, you . . . you big fibber!'

Rhona's face sets from the chin up; the mouth, the cheeks, until her shining eyes are all that seem alive.

'I didn't say I was getting a *new* one!'

'*Fibber*! I bet you've got my coat too!'

Rhona recoils as if she has been punched.

'Well, if that's what you think, you can go home *now*!'

'I will, then!'

Melanie crosses to the top of the ladder. For a second, Rhona blocks her way.

'Melanie! The bell was for you. It was *your* present!'

Melanie shakes her head. She pushes past and shins down the ladder until she can look up at Rhona's pink legs, the scraped knees under her skirt. Suddenly the day before seems shameful and dangerous and very long ago.

'You can send my coat back when you find it,' she hisses, and Rhona screams and stamps at Melanie's finger; but Melanie is away, running down the stairs, passing Rhona's mother.

'Hello!' purrs Mrs Knox. 'Playing chase, are you?' She hugs the idea to her bosom like a bouquet and sings, 'Coming! Ready or not!'

Melanie decides that, when she gets home, she will tell them that Rhona's mother is cuckoo and that Rhona is a thief.

Melanie's brown beret is too tight and she knows that, when she takes it off, her hair will be set in two layers like a cottage loaf. She tugs at her yellow neckerchief. It's strange to be in the school hall on a Saturday, with the smell of hymn books and stewed dinners still lingering. Mrs Price's piano is shrouded in the corner, cannily turned to the wall so that no one will try to sit on it.

Melanie's Brownie outfit, in contrast to her usual school uniform, feels like playing in an 'away' strip. She's not sure she likes it, the way it mutes her individuality; earlier, a woman she didn't even know stopped her and pulled her socks up. Other Brownies appear here and there in the unusual adult crowd. They are all eating, all the time: home-made fairy cakes and scones, gingerbread men with mutilated limbs. Melanie's mother didn't bake anything, but she will be coming down later with a bag of old clothes for the second-hand stall. In deference to Mrs Alexander, she has been washing and ironing them all week; the *really* old clothes, the shameful ones, have been relegated to work duty. Melanie's father has been wearing them, digging the flower beds over for Spring like a scarecrow gardener.

Most of the Brownies are in chatty gaggles, but Melanie sells raffle tickets alone. She is shy of talking to the other girls' parents and she has sold only six. Two of those she bought herself, although she has no interest in winning the *Half a Lamb, Courtesy of Fate and Son, Family Butchers,* or in the 'Humpty' *Family! Knitted by the Ladies of the Mothers' Union.* She has seen the Humpty Family; they look as if they have waddled out of a nightmare.

Her mother comes into the hall, embarrassingly smart in a camel coat and lipstick. She looks awkward, not sure of the etiquette of carrying a large bin bag. Melanie swerves through the crowd to get to her, tugs on her arm.

'Mam, will you buy some raffle tickets off me? I've only sold six.'

'In a minute. I said, *in a minute*, Melanie! Where's Mrs Alexander? Ah.' Click click of her heels on the waxed parquet.

Melanie hates her mother's social face, the cringe and twang in her voice when she talks to Mrs Alexander.

'Hell-oh, Barbara! Doesn't it all look lovely?'

Mrs Alexander, who spends so much of her time with little girls, speaks to everyone like a child.

'Well! Haven't you brought a big bag? Well done! Let's see what we've got . . .'

Melanie's mother tips the bag out, smiling proudly at the crispness of her ironing and the smell of the extra conditioner that she put in the wash. Melanie reaches out to stroke one of her own baby bonnets: the soft yellow wool, the silky ribbons. She's amazed to think that she was ever that small, that her mother could hold her whole self in her arms. She delves further among the bootees and cardigans and scarves and, underneath it all, she finds her old coat.

Melanie looks up but her mother is smirking into Mrs Alexander's face, nodding at something she says. She looks down again, gripping the edge of the trestle table, and the clothes seem to rustle and crawl. It is, it really is her coat, the one that went missing, and the sudden host of ideas makes her feel sick. Her mother looks down at her at last.

'For goodness' sake, Melanie! What's wrong with you?' she says, and then: 'Ah.'

Driving home, it starts to rain. Melanie takes the raffle tickets, warm from her pocket, and folds them; not even seven times, only four. She rips them into confetti and pushes them into the plastic ashtray in the door of the car.

Swishing along the wet street, they pass Rhona pedalling grimly up the hill. She wears a coat like a big cape and it parachutes out behind her. The bike sways with the effort of her pumping legs. Melanie's mother would normally say something on seeing Rhona, and Melanie would normally say something in agreement. But Melanie is not speaking to her mother. She draws circles and squares and shields on the steamy window; then she wipes them off with her yellow neckerchief. With the sound of the rain and the wipers' regular, two-note clunk, she is not sure if she heard the ring of a bicycle bell.

The Hanged Man

By Ian Rankin

The killer wandered through the fairground.

It was a travelling fair, and this was its first night in Kirkcaldy. It was a Thursday evening in April. The fair wouldn't get really busy until the weekend, by which time it would be missing one of its minor, if well-established, attractions.

He'd already made one recce past the small white caravan with its chalkboard outside. Pinned to the board were a couple of faded letters from satisfied customers. A double-step led to the bead curtain. The door was tied open with baling-twine. He didn't think there was anyone in there with her. If there was, she'd have closed the door. But all the same, he wanted to be careful. 'Care' was his by-word.

He called himself a killer. Which was to say that if anyone had asked him what he did for a living, he wouldn't have used any other term. He knew some in the profession thought 'assassin' had a more glamorous ring to it. He'd looked it up in a dictionary, found it was to do with some old religious sect and derived from an old Arabic word meaning 'eater of hashish'. He didn't believe in drugs himself; not so much as a half of lager before the job.

Some people preferred to call it a 'hit', which made them 'hitmen'. But he didn't *hit* people; he killed them stone dead. And there were other, more obscure euphemisms, but the bottom line was, he was a killer.

And for today, the fair was his place of work, his hunting ground.

Not that it had taken a magic ball to find the subject. She'd be in that caravan right now, waiting for a punter. He'd give it ten more minutes, just so he could be sure she wasn't with someone – not a punter necessarily; maybe sharing a cuppa with a fellow traveller. Ten minutes; if no one came out or went in, he'd make himself her next and final customer.

Of course, if she was a real astrologer, she'd know he was coming and would have high-tailed it out of town. But he thought she was here. He *knew* she was.

He pretended to watch three youths on the firing-range. They made the elementary mistake of aiming along the barrel. The sights, of course, had been skewed; probably the barrel, too. And if they thought they were going to dislodge one of the moving targets by hitting it . . . well, best think again. Those targets would be weighted, reinforced. The odds were always on the side of the showman.

The market stretched along the waterfront. There was a stiff breeze making some of the wooden structures creak. People pushed hair out of their eyes, or tucked chins into the collars of their jackets. The place wasn't busy, but it was busy enough. He didn't stand out, nothing memorable about him at all. His jeans, lumberjack shirt and trainers were work clothes; at home he preferred a bit more style. But he was a long way from home today. His base was on the west coast, just down the Clyde from Glasgow. He didn't know anything about Fife at all. Kirkcaldy, what little he'd seen of it, wouldn't be lingering in his memory. He'd been to towns all over Scotland and the North of England. In his mind they formed a geography of violence. In Carlisle he'd used a knife, making it look like a drunken Saturday brawl. In Peterhead it had been a blow to the head and strangulation, with orders that the body shouldn't ever be found – a grand and a half to a fishing-boat captain had seen to that. In Airdrie, Arbroath, Ardrossan . . . he didn't always kill. Sometimes all that was needed was a brutal and public message. In those cases he became the postman, delivering the message to order.

He moved from the shooting-range to another stall, where children tried to attach hoops to the prizes on a carousel. They were faring little better than their elders next door. No surprise, with most of the prizes oh-so-slightly exceeding the circumference of each hoop. When he checked his watch, he was surprised to find that the ten minutes had passed. A final look around, and he climbed the steps, tapped at the open door and parted the bead curtain.

'Come in, love,' she said. Gypsy Rosa, the sign outside called her. Palms read, your fortune foretold. Yet here she was, waiting for him.

'Close the door,' she instructed. He saw that the twine holding it open was looped over a bent nail. He loosed it and closed the door. The curtains were shut – which was ideal for his purpose – and, lacking any light from outside, the interior glowed from the half-dozen candles spaced around it. The surfaces had been draped with lengths of cheap black cloth. There was a black cloth over the table, too, with patterns of sun and moon embroidered into it. And there she sat, gesturing for him to squeeze his large frame into the banquette opposite. He nodded. He smiled. He looked at her.

She was middle-aged, her face lined and rouged. She'd been a looker in younger days, he could see that, but scarlet lipstick now made her mouth look too large and moist. She wore black muslin over her head, a gold band holding it in place. Her costume looked authentic enough: black lace, red silk, with astrological signs sewn into the arms. On the table sat a crystal ball, covered for now with a white handkerchief. The red fingernails of one hand tapped against a tarot deck. She asked him his name.

'Is that necessary?' he asked.

She shrugged. 'It helps sometimes.' They were like blind dates alone in a restaurant, the world outside ceasing to matter. Her eyes twinkled in the candlelight.

'My name's Mort,' he told her.

She repeated the name, seeming amused by it.

'Short for Morton. My father was born there.'

'It's also the French for death,' she added.

'I didn't know,' he lied.

She was smiling. 'There's a lot you don't know, Mort. That's why you're here. A palm-reading, is it?'

'What else do you offer?'

'The ball.' She nodded towards it. 'The cards.'

He asked which she would recommend. In turn, she asked if this was his first visit to a psychic healer – that's what she called herself, 'a psychic healer': 'because I heal souls', she added by way of explanation.

'I'm not sure I need healing,' he argued.

'Oh, my dear, we all need some kind of healing. We're none of us *whole*. Look at you, for example.'

He straightened in his chair, becoming aware for the first time that she was holding his right hand, palm upwards, her fingers stroking his knuckles. She looked down at the palm, frowned a little in concentration.

'You're a visitor, aren't you, dear?'

'Yes.'

'Here on business, I'd say.'

'Yes.' He was studying the palm with her, as though trying to read its foreign words.

'Mmm.' She began running the tip of one finger down the well-defined lines which criss-crossed his palm. 'Not ticklish?' she chuckled. He allowed her the briefest of smiles. Looking at her face, he noticed it seemed softer than it had when he'd first entered the caravan. He revised her age downwards, felt slight pressure as she seemed to squeeze his hand, as if acknowledging the compliment.

'Doing all right for yourself, though,' she informed him. 'I mean moneywise; no problems there. No, dear, *your* problems all stem from your particular line of work.'

'My work?'

'You're not as relaxed about it as you used to be. Time was, you wouldn't have considered doing anything else. Easy money. But it doesn't feel like that any more, does it?'

It felt warm in the caravan, stuffy, with no air getting in and all those candles burning. There was the metal weight pressed to his groin, the weight he'd always found so reassuring in times past. He told himself she was using cheap psychology. His accent wasn't local; he wore no wedding-ring; his hands were clean and manicured. You could tell a lot about someone from such details.

'Shouldn't we agree a price first?' he asked.

'Why should we do that, dear? I'm not a prostitute, am I?' He felt his ears reddening. 'And besides, you can afford it, we both know you can. What's the point of letting money get in the way?' She was holding his hand in an ever tighter grip. She had strength, this one; he'd bear that in mind when the time came. He wouldn't play around, wouldn't string out her suffering. A quick squeeze of the trigger.

'I get the feeling', she said, 'you're wondering why you're here. Would that be right?'

'I know exactly why I'm here.'

'What? Here with me? Or here on this planet, living the life you've chosen?'

'Either . . . both.' He spoke a little too quickly, could feel his pulse-rate rising. He had to get it down again, had to be calm when the time came. Part of him said *Do it now*. But another part said *Hear her out*. He wriggled, trying to get comfortable.

'What I meant though', she went on, 'is you're not sure any more why you do what you do. You've started to ask questions.' She looked up at him. 'The line of business you're in, I get the feeling you're just supposed to do what you're told. Is that right?' He nodded. 'No talking back, no questions asked. You just do your work and wait for payday.'

'I get paid upfront.'

'Aren't you the lucky one?' She chuckled again. 'But the money's not enough, is it? It can never recompense for not being happy or fulfilled.'

'I could have got that from my girlfriend's *Cosmopolitan*.'

She smiled, then clapped her hands. 'I'd like to try you with the cards. Are you game?'

'Is that what this is – a game?'

'You have your fun with words, dear. Euphemisms, that's all words are.'

He tried not to gasp; it was as if she'd read his mind from earlier – all those euphemisms for 'killer'. She wasn't paying him any heed, was busy shuffling the outsized tarot deck. She asked him to touch the deck three times. Then she laid out the top three cards.

'Ah,' she said, her fingers caressing the first one. '*Le soleil.* It means the sun.'

'I know what it means,' he snapped.

She made a pout with her lips. 'I thought you didn't know any French.'

He was stuck for a moment. 'There's a picture of the sun right there on the card,' he said finally.

She nodded slowly. His breathing had quickened again.

'Second card,' she said. 'Death himself. *La mort.* Interesting that the French give it the feminine gender.'

He looked at the picture of the skeleton. It was grinning, doing a little jig. On the ground beside it sat a lantern and an hourglass. The candle in the lantern had been snuffed out; the sand in the hourglass had all fallen through.

'Don't worry,' she said, 'it doesn't always portend a death.'

'That's a relief,' he said with a smile.

'The final card is intriguing – the hanged man. It can signify many things.' She lifted it up so he could see it.

'And the three together?' he asked, curious now.

She held her hands as if in prayer. 'I'm not sure,' she said at last. 'An unusual conjunction, to be sure.'

'Death and the hanged man: a suicide maybe?'

She shrugged.

'Is the sex important? I mean, the fact that it *is* a man?'

She shook her head.

He licked his lips. 'Maybe the ball would help,' he suggested.

She looked at him, her eyes reflecting light from the candles. 'You might be right.' And she smiled. 'Shall we?' As if they were not prospective lovers now but children, and the crystal ball little more than an illicit dare.

As she pulled the small glass globe towards them, he shifted again. The pistol barrel was chafing his thigh. He rubbed his jacket pocket, the one containing the silencer. He would have to hit her first, just to quiet her while he fitted the silencer to the gun.

Slowly, she lifted the handkerchief from the ball, as if raising the curtain on some miniaturised stage-show. She leaned forward, peering into the glass, giving him a view of crêped cleavage. Her hands flitted over the ball, not quite touching it. Had he been a gerontophile, there would have been a hint of the erotic to the act.

'Don't you go thinking that!' she snapped. Then, seeing the startled look on his face, she winked. 'The ball often makes things clearer.'

'What was I thinking?' he blurted out.

'You want me to say it out loud?'

He shook his head, looked into the ball, saw her face reflected there, stretched and distorted. And floating somewhere within was his own face, too, surrounded by licking flames.

'What do you see?' he asked, needing to know now.

'I see a man who is asking why he is here. One person has the answer, but he has yet to ask this person. He is worried about the thing he must do – rightly worried, in my opinion.'

She looked up at him again. Her eyes were the colour of polished oak. Tiny veins of blood seemed to pulse in the whites. He jerked back in his seat.

'You know, don't you?'

'Of course I know, Mort.'

He nearly overturned the table as he got to his feet, pulling the gun from his waistband. 'How?' he asked. 'Who told you?'

She shook her head, not looking at the gun, apparently not interested in it. 'It would happen one day. The moment you walked in, I felt it was you.'

'You're not afraid.' It was a statement rather than a question.

'Of course I'm afraid.' But she didn't look it. 'And a little sad, too.'

He had the silencer out of his pocket, but was having trouble coordinating his hands. He'd practised a hundred times in the dark and had never had this trouble before. He'd had victims like her, though: the ones who accepted, who were maybe even a little grateful.

'You know who wants you dead?' he asked.

She nodded. 'I think so. I may have gotten the odd fortune wrong but I've made precious few enemies in my life.'

'He's a rich man.'

'Very rich,' she conceded. Not all of it honest money. And I'm sure he's well used to getting what he wants.' She slid the ball away, brought out the cards again and began shuffling them. 'So ask me your question.'

He was screwing the silencer on to the end of the barrel. The pistol was loaded, he only had to slide the safety off. He licked his lips again. So hot in here, so dry . . .

'Why?' he asked. 'Why does he want a fortune-teller dead?'

She got up, made to open the curtains.

'No.' he commanded, pointing the gun at her, sliding off the safety. 'Keep them closed.'

'Afraid to shoot me in daylight?' When he didn't answer, she pulled open one curtain, then blew out the candles. He kept the pistol trained on her: a head shot, quick and always fatal. 'I'll tell you,' she said, sliding into her seat again. She motioned for him to sit. After a moment's hesitation he did so, the pistol steady in his right hand. Wisps of smoke from the extinguished candles rose either side of her.

'We were young when we met,' she began. I was already working in a fairground – not this one. One night, he decided there had been enough of a courtship.' She looked deep into his eyes, his own oak-coloured eyes. 'Oh yes, he's used to getting what he wants. You know what I'm saying?' she went on quietly. 'There was no question of consent. I tried to have the baby in secret, but it's hard to keep secrets from a man like him, a man with money, someone people fear. My baby was stolen from me. I began travelling then, and I've been travelling ever since. But always with my ear to the ground, always hearing things.' Her eyes were liquid now. 'You see, I knew a time would come when my baby would grow old enough to begin asking questions. And I knew the baby's father would not want the truth to come out.' She reached out a shaking hand, reached past the gun to touch his cheek. 'I just didn't think he'd be so cruel.'

'Cruel?'

'So cruel as to send his own son – our son – to do his killing.'

He shot to his feet again, banged his fists against the wall of the caravan. Rested his head there and screwed shut his eyes, the oak-coloured eyes –

mirrors of her own – which had told her all she'd needed to know. He'd left the pistol on the table. She lifted it, surprised by its weight, and turned it in her hand.

'I'll kill him,' he groaned. 'I swear, I'll kill him for this.'

With a smile, she slid the safety catch on, placed the gun back on the table. When he turned back to her, blinking away tears, she looked quite calm, almost serene, as if her faith in him had been rewarded at last. In her hand, she was holding a tarot card.

The hanged man.

'It will need to look like an accident,' she said. 'Either that or suicide.'

Outside, the screams of frightened children: waltzers and big wheel and ghost train. One of his hands fell lightly on hers, the other reaching for his pistol.

'Mother,' he said, with all the tenderness his parched soul could muster.

Elizabeth Reeder lives and works in Glasgow. Her story Crosswords *was shortlisted for the 1998 Macallan/Scotland on Sunday* Short Story Competition. *Common* Knowledge *is the first crime story she has ever written. She wishes the story was fiction, but reality hit home when a woman was drug-raped in Glasgow while she was finishing the last draft. This story is for her.*

Common Knowledge

By Elizabeth Reeder

His face is unremarkable. He lives next door, he works beside you, he stands at the bar and does not say much. His hair is blond, sometimes jet-black and all the shades between. He is short, skinny, tall and fat. He flirts with blue eyes and laughs with the depth of brown. He is handsome and has some serious personality flaws. He is successful and smart. He has a small scar above his eyebrow. He could be considered perfect. He is out of work and prone to be a bit rash because of it. He might be a bit slow but is into power, control and a little bit on the side. He is used to getting his own way. He looks familiar in that Joe Bloggs kind of way. You'll know him when you see him. Try to remember his face.

Reality is, after all, what you remember. He told me that I would forget. And I did.

Today is the day after and what I remember of my life is a reassuring unbroken black line from what has been until what is now – reassuring except for yesterday's eight missing hours. What I remember of yesterday is the first bitter taste of my coffee, the church bells chiming four o'clock and his face turned towards the light. I remember little else until the shine of his teeth in the sun wakes me up, middle of the night, sweat drenched. And Jules holds me in that night, knowing more than me. Hands moving rhythmically, predictably through my hair. Warm words soothing into my sleep-cushioned ear. Her hand worrying on the spot on my arm where there will be a bruise.

I have forgotten time, how my cup was emptied, which questions I asked him and then I remember the jolt of shock as his fingers broke the skin of my arm. He held me with violence so that I would know that he was not going to let me go. He knew that his nails digging into my skin would be enough to shift me into reality. And the digging did shift me into the moment like sheet lightening, brilliant against the dark of storm skies. Then it passed so quick that I wonder if it happened at all.

I do not remember what happened between walking into the café and waking up, startled by the white shock of his teeth, in my own bed.

And to know that I am not alone in this not remembering. This is not a nineties thing, not really. We always lose memory along the way. Trauma, old age, human nature. We cannot blame drink or drugs, not here, not ever.

But imagine yourself. Stone sober or after a few drinks. It does not matter. You will be lucid before it begins. He may buy you a drink, chat you up, tell you all about himself. Or he might never show his face; you might go for a dance or toss your head back in laughter and your drink is different after. But you cannot see or taste the difference. Either way, after fifteen minutes you will have trouble walking, following a thought through to completion. You will need to be steadied as you walk. To strangers you will look blind drunk, out of it, letting walls hold you up, talking, but without a shred of memory to tie moments together. This is what he is after.

He is after the oblivion you are in. He will take you there, take you then and you will not remember his hands, your voice saying no, the walk home. You will be absent for hours and since you don't know, or don't know for sure, you can't really speak. You don't know what to say. *I think, maybe, I have a feeling that* . . . If it is only these snapshots, or a sick feeling, you could be making it all up. Women do that, make things up; everyone knows that. This is his best defence: misinformation, misogyny and the sporadic nature of remembrances.

Over the next few years you will remember more and more and you will know what he did to you and you will be able to do nothing. Hearsay. He says. She says.

I phoned the paper on a Thursday. They put me through to her directly. The article had come out on the Monday and it was making my life awkward. She printed my name. I could take her to court for that. Rumours, nothing proven and my name right there. Small-time paper, small circulation but right there in black and white: my name and a physical description so exact that it could almost have been a photograph. Some colleagues look at me strangely; one or two have slapped me with congratulations on the shoulders. Impressed. I joke back but know that this rumour is dangerous.

I phoned her to arrange a meeting and clear my name. She will believe me, I have that kind of face. She is out of her league. She writes for the food page for Christ's sake. She must have bribed someone to get the tiny article on to the women's pages. She wrote it because I supposedly raped her sister. She wrote it as a warning of sorts: my name, details of a few women's stories, some sketchy details about the drug. Nothing proven or even provable.

When we meet I will charm her and convince her how untrue the rumours are, how women don't always remember things very well. I will tell this woman, Fiona, that the women made passes at me, that I never used a drug, that women will say anything, that I never raped anyone. That it is simple: attraction, repulsion and regret. They all consented, then regretted. How can they remember my face if they remember little else? Maybe I will tell her that it was not me at all. It does not matter. By the end of the meeting she will know nothing of substance but she will know that I am not her man. She will print a retraction. If not I will take her to court.

I had never seen him before I walked into the sunny and busy café. He had told me on the phone that he would be sitting by the window and, with a hint of anger, that I already knew what he looked like as I had put a description in the article. He sits looking out the window with his face tilted toward the afternoon-angled light. His face at rest is not particularly friendly but when he smiles at me in recognition he is credible in the space between curved lips.

His blond hair sticks up in short thickly gelled spikes. His thick neck is a brief sneeze between broad shoulders and a round head. His muscular legs are crammed into oversized jeans and he sits with his legs open, a testament to what he has. He has freckles from the sun rather than youth and something about the way he sits makes me think that when he speaks he will not be eloquent, but exact. He looks classically handsome, awe-inspiring, or at least he would like to think. I nod to him and think about how silly and uninformed these classics are.

I had an open mind when I walked through the door. While I was sure that there was a man out there using a drug to rape women, I was not sure that he would be the one. His call was so unusual, his anger about having his name printed so strong, that I thought that I could be mistaken. That he could be innocent. However, when I see him for the first time I know that he is the one. I know that he seeks out women in clubs. This knowledge gives me the shivers.

I go over to the counter and order my coffee from a smooth-faced university student. She looks between him and me and blinks with long lashes. I see her look through me, her mind wandering. I am thinking about the questions I will ask. My hands are steady but my heart beats quickly, my stomach churns, threatens revolt.

She picks up a dishwasher-warm mug and clicks freshly ground coffee into the filter. Her eyes scan the café as she tilts and pushes the tight metal of the group arm into its socket and places the mug beneath the nozzle. She froths the milk, looking at me and the wall behind with equal interest. I take my coffee and with a smile and thanks I pop a tip into the mug on the counter and walk to the table.

The church bells chime out each chord of four o'clock. He listens to the bells and waits for the ringing in my ears to stop. Not just the bells but that lingering echo after they finish. It feels almost like he is inside the bells and my head. I cannot tell if the bells please or unnerve him. In this true silence he turns towards me. His eyes move across my face like hands over braille taking me in like words; a dot dropped, lost and found. He looks bored and calm.

He opens his shoulders, *You must be Fiona. A pleasure.* He tilts his head in slight reverence and offers me a solid hand. I nod and smile but refuse his offering.

I make a mental note about the bells. I make only a mental note because as I start to write in my notebook his hand forbids me to write anything. No notes. A simple unchallengeable statement. I am at a loss. I look at him and then out of the window. I know that if I push him he will walk out of the café and I cannot let that happen because I am here to find a way to bring him down. I look out the window at the church and the women passing by. I am aware that they do not know what he has done, would not know how to protect themselves. How many women already? I had guessed eight. Eight women including my sister Sally. For Sally I remain where I am. I take a sip of my coffee and know that I will not take any notes but do my best to keep him here and talking.

Questions? I have questions written down, can I reference those? He slides the notebook over to his side and starts to go through the pages. He begins to shift through my pencilled notes and I feel the panic rise, starting at my toes, but I stop it at the curve of my knees. My voice comes out calm. *The last page. I've written them on the back of the last page.* His eyes turn up towards me, I swear that he is almost grinning. He turns the notebook over and opens the back cover. There they are, eleven questions neatly printed in black ink. He reads the list and asks me why I have used pen for the questions and pencil for the rest. *Pen for questions, pencil for answers. Because I am always more sure of the questions.* He smiles again, slides the notebook back to me and begins to answer the first question without prompting.

Why did I phone you? Easy, because you have the wrong man. His voice falls out in shorthand: smooth phrases, gruff exclamations and sentences which are never left hanging. He regularly pauses as he searches for the right word, and it is always exactly the right word. And sometimes I feel that the search is a show put on for me.

The rumours which led you to contact me are silly, pernicious. It was never me. You really want to find someone else. Those things that were done to those women could never be me.

I try to listen and follow what he says which, as far as I can tell, is nothing of any relevance. By the time his coffee is cooled, mine is finished and I do not know a thing.

When she walks in I know what I have to do. She is out of her depth but thinks herself capable. She is so sure that she has the right guy. So sure that she can bring me down. She needs taking down a notch. She thinks of herself as untouchable. Probably has some bitch at home too. Looks the type. She walks in and orders her coffee and she thinks that she is beyond my power of persuasion. I put my hand into my pocket and slid a pill between my thumb and forefinger. I have never used it in a café before but it is busy and the risk thrills me. When she sits down I turn on the charm, become the perfect interviewee, then I stop her from writing. She has a moment of loss. In the moment when her guard drops and she decides whether she really wants to be here at this table with me, I make my move. I move fast.

I place my hand back along the smooth white porcelain cup with a handle too small for an adult hand. I have drunk nearly half but now as it cools I make no move to drink it, only to circle its rim, fancying to myself that it might hum like a champagne glass if I were to test for friction. I resolve not to give into my desire for noise and watch as her eyes go distant, as she repeats the same question that she asked five minutes ago.

She walks through the door, gives a small wave of acknowledgement to the familiar-looking man sitting by the window and orders a latte. She looks at me boldly but fear shifts behind her eyes. In her hand she holds a heavy A4 wirebound notebook with a red pencil held criss-crossed against the black cover. I make her coffee, trying to read her. The tables are emptying, the beginning of one of the many five-minute lulls during the day. They never last long. After I serve her I will clear some of the cups and plates. I wonder why they are meeting. They look like a disparate couple. She does not look the type to go for a man, much less a rugby player with a neck like that and a face to match.

He is intent on the sounds outside. As I walk near the table he turns to the woman, smiles, says her name and offers her his hand. She kindly declines. His smile goes even broader, meticulous white teeth gleaming. I know that smile.

I wipe down the table behind her, pick up lingering cups, and his eyes move over me, around my edges like an etching, and then away. He doesn't seem to know who I am. I must be mistaking him for someone else. A group of five have come in the door. I go behind the counter to serve them.

When she starts to repeat herself I begin to have fun. How are you feeling, Fiona? She smiles, says fine and looks at her notebook and tries to figure out which question she is on. I tell her how I persuade women to have sex. I tell her that I have popped a pill into the coffee she has just finished. I tell her that she is next. I smile and laugh and she joins me. She can remember no joke but laughs anyway.

I place my hand on her leg beneath the table. A slow inch up her thigh. Her eyes spit terror, then nothing-her brain forgets too quickly. I remove my hand and compliment her. I tell her that I am going to fuck her and then I compliment her hair. I tell her that I like women who say no. Does she want another coffee? She says no, misses the irony. I place my hand on hers, circling my finger on her palm. She looks around for a second in panic and then she forgets to be afraid and relaxes. I let go. I tell her that I have raped sixteen women, not the eight she put in the article. I comment on the colours of the evening coming in, that I will make it hurt, that she will forget, that bells remind me of Hemingway. I tell her that she will remember just enough for it to bother her for the rest of her life. I tell her that no one will believe her, that she has beautiful eyes. That I wear a condom and leave nothing behind. That nothing is going to happen.

The bells ring again. Five o'clock. Something focuses for a second behind her eyes and she asks a question which is not written down. She asks a question because she knows that I am the one.

But why do you do it? Why? I have never really thought about that before. *Why? Because I can. Because I have this drug that takes away their ability to resist. Because these women deserve it. Because you deserve it. Their attitudes, their slickness, the way they look right through me.* I look at her, drugged as she is, and how she still believes herself to be out of reach. *I rape women because they think that they are beyond the small horrors of life. They think that they are too good for me. Because there is a thrill to be able to do what I want, to women who don't want it. Because I did it and got away with it. Memory, my dear Fiona, is the crux of all prosecutions. And memory is exactly what they do not have. Article or no article, you are fighting a losing battle. You've lost.*

I decide that it is time to leave. Since she walked in that door I knew that she would leave with me. She needs my help to stand. She looks drunk and in need of support. I lift her up and let my fingers dig into her arms. I pull her towards me in an embrace. Feel the curve of her breasts against me, this will be good. Then I move behind her so that I can lean her into my chest. I place my other arm around her waist. I smile and tell her that I am going to take her somewhere where no one will hear a thing.

I watch them talk. He smiles a lot and she responds. He places his hand on her leg beneath the table. It makes me feel uncomfortable. I am sure that I have seen her on the scene before, that her girlfriend is a short, square woman with great dimples. An engineer or something. Not that some of us don't go both ways but she really doesn't seem the type.

I serve customers with my usual efficiency but find myself watching the table. I walk by a few times to see if I can remember who he is. He is often pushed in close to her, almost whispering. I figure that it will come to me in a few days. Maybe a friend of my brother's or something.

At five my shift is over and I am getting ready to go but I don't leave. I hover behind the counter serving a few extra customers. He gets up to go. He pulls her up beside him. She is having trouble standing. One hand is grabbing her arm, the other is around her waist. It almost looks romantic. She gives out a small cry of pain. He smiles. I know that smile.

Between them. I knock over a coffee on my way out from behind the counter. I have to get between them and the door. I try to remember the name he said. No time. Fffff. I guess.

Fiona? His eyes blink, I have it right. *Where are you going? You said that you were going to stay and have a coffee with me on my break. I has been such a long time, this is such a great coincidence.* I have taken her notebook and then her other arm. I address the man, who I now remember enough to know that she will not be leaving with him; *she used to date my older brother, years ago.* Fiona looks at him and then me and does not recognise either one of us. She is a puppet between us, unable to figure out why we each have an arm. I look at him. He knows that I know who he is. I know that he remembers me too. The bastard. I want to punch him. It takes all my energy not to do so. I need to stop him from taking her out the door. Punching him will not do any good.

Trouble fires into the air, people have stopped talking and are looking in our direction. A couple of people point, recognising him. I remember him too. That article in the paper last week. He is an exact match. I begin to lead her back into the café. His hand continues to squeeze her arm. I tell him to let go or I will begin to yell his name and what he does to women. He feels all the eyes on him, knows that I will make a scene. I have never heard such an edge to my voice. He releases her arm. *I'll see you later, Fiona, it was good talking with you.* He takes her hand and she shakes. He gives me a look like a threat and walks through the door. I take her to the back room. She is calm, oblivious, muttering on about bells. I am shaking uncontrollably.

They say memory loss compounds trauma.

The day after, I report the incident to the police (the woman from the café, Karen, helps me to fill in details), give them a urine sample and tell them what drug to look for. They look at me in disbelief, knowing that I have made it all up. I know that they have had at least six other women report similar circumstances in the last four months. I realise that the world has not caught up with reality yet. Drug or no drug, the incident is no-crimed.

A week later I am still waking up in the middle of the night, the gap in my memory filled with violent absences. Jules holds me and tells me that I am safe. I do not feel safe. Not here, not outside. I thought that I had better judgement. My arm is sore and visible but I know that other things happened. Could have happened. What must Sally and the rest feel? Everyone just thought that they were drunk, out of sorts. No one saved them. They can't remember and until you lose your memory you don't know how terrifying it can be. You do not know what he did, what you did, how you survived. It can be worse than knowing for sure. Your body remembers, it knows, and you just can't make it real in your head.

You have eight women, sixteen women, hundreds of women who do not remember. You have one, twenty, one hundred guilty men who do. At some point you realise that the remembering is not the problem, it's not knowing what to do to silence the voices of terror in your own head. It's not knowing what to do to stop them from raping other women.

A plan begins to emerge. When I was in university we used to put information about known rapists on the mirrors of women's toilets. All women spend at least a little time looking in the mirror and word got around. We told each other what we knew and it seemed to help.

I try to write another article but they will not print it because I have no proof and he got all of his mates to call in to complain about the first one. Instead I tell the story to everyone I know. I buy some air time and make his name and what he has done common knowledge. Rumour has it that he is going to take me to court for destroying his good name.

I continue on, committed to my cause, ceaseless in how my mouth moves, telling truths. I begin to place my trust in word of mouth. Hearsay. She says and she says and she says.

Manda Scott is a veterinary surgeon, writer and climber. Originally from Glasgow, she lives currently in Suffolk with a growing family of lurchers and cats. Her first novel, Hen's Teeth, *was shortlisted for the 1997 Orange Prize; her second,* Night Mares, *was published in 1998. A third is in press and a fourth under way.*

Of Tooth and Claw

By Manda Scott

Fur coats are worn by beautiful animals and ugly people. It was printed on the T-shirts we wore at college. A dozen of us, ardent in our belief that, by protest, we could change the world. We painted our banners and we threw the unused paint across the windscreens of those who might, conceivably, once have worn something of animal origin, safe in the knowledge that, by this, we would persuade them to change. We were young, you understand, and knew nothing of the real world: of commerce and politics, of lobbying and brown paper envelopes. All we knew was that feeling led to action and that action brought results. It was a good time to be young. Now I am older and I know better. Now I live in the wood and for the wood and I understand rather more of the ways of the world. Listen and I will tell you the reality.

In the beginning, it was hard. You can spend half of your life reading underground magazines, going to workshops, visiting web-sites, gathering every whisker of potentially useful information but when the reality hits, living off the land is never quite the rustic idyll they all proclaim. Living off the land and staying invisible while you do it is twice as hard and so it was well over a month before I wandered far enough from the bender to find the farm. It was a grey, cold, frost-bitten Spring morning, some time after the new moon and before the equinoctial gales. It rained overnight and there was a leak in the bender and I spent the dark hours before dawn running spit-wet fingers down the internal struts to make a path for the water. They teach you that at the workshops. It works, I can tell you, in a tipi in the Nebraska desert. It works less well in this land in March. The first few runnels of water did, indeed, follow the line of my spit down the long shanks of hazel. A hoop of water formed on the bare earth at the edge of my groundsheet, a living testament to the ingenuity of my teachers. Later, though, as other leaks showed up, gravity chose the more direct route and a small river flowed out on to my sleeping bag. Later still a second deluge found my spare set of jeans. Later even than that, the sky cleared and the temperature dropped and everything that had been wet but warm became wet and very, very cold. It never happened like that in Nebraska.

I was not, you might understand, in the best frame of mind by the time the sun came up with the thaw. I abandoned the bender as soon as it was light enough to see and I went for a walk. I walked to keep warm, I walked to keep time to my internal dialogue, I walked to find something to eat beyond the rabbits and the fish and the fungi. I walked new paths to new places and when I had walked further than the morning would allow and the sun had moved round to the afternoon, I stopped walking and I just stood and looked.

I was looking at a farm. A factory farm with long rows of wire cages, each one of them heaving with life. A farm that smelled: stronger than fox, stronger than badger, stronger even than the stoat that hunts the warren behind the bender. If the wind had been blowing the other way, I would have smelled it before I saw it. As it was, the stench hit me like a wall, just before the noise, and I would be hard pushed, now, to say which of them was worse. You can hold your nose to the smell but the sound sank into my soul and I don't think it will ever come out: a soft, sibilant chittering, like the communing of ghosts, and over it all the short, sharp eruptions that are the tearing of new-dead flesh.

There were men there when I saw it first. Men in overalls hosing out the cages. Men in suits filling in forms. Men in donkey jackets waiting around to drive the trucks that brought in the food. They used wire winches to unload the carcasses and you could identify the bodies by their feet: the solid round hoofs of the horses, the cloven dinner plates of the cattle, the neat pointed toes of sheep or goats. This time last year they would have been feeding fish, but the bottom has fallen out of the meat markets and they can feed what they like to their inmates and still make a profit. You will wonder perhaps that they didn't see me but they were not tight on security, then. They thought that seclusion made for protection and that what the public didn't know wasn't going to hurt them. If you bear in mind that they'd been there for nigh on fifteen years, then it's fair to say they were right. But not for long.

It's odd the things that change your perspective. I spent most of that morning cursing the cold, the gods and myself, in more or less that order, and walking fast to keep warm. I spent most of the evening sitting as still as was humanly possible, the cold and the gods forgotten, making an internal inventory of every move on the farm. This is the kind of thing they were training us for in Nebraska, the long day's watch of the enemy. I backed off only once, in the late evening, to empty my bladder and by the time I came back, the only one left was the Suit with the clipboards and the mobile phone grafted to his ear. I wasn't bothering to hide by then, it was close to dark and he didn't have eyes for the trees. He was planning a tryst with his mistress and lying to his wife and checking the fuel gauge in the Mercedes to make sure he was going to be able to see both without making the detour to fill up en route. He drove out without locking the gates and that, you see, was just such a terribly bad mistake.

It was a silver mink farm. Or, rather, a farm for silver mink. Thousands upon thousands of them, sharp of tooth and claw, stuffing their little faces with the throwaway products of our slaughter houses, the zero profits of our farms, growing fat and sleek and soft-pelted and then breeding like rabbits to produce more happy mink. Of course, you couldn't say, as such, that they were happy but I have to tell you that, having been there and walked down between the rows, they didn't seem to me to be unduly pissed off with life. They hadn't, after all, spent the night in a leaking bender watching the frost grow up the walls.

I went home that night, to eat and sleep and think on it. The gods were good and the rain stopped and the following morning was warm enough to inspire a bit of DIY. I fixed the leaks in the roof and then walked into the village for a shower at the youth hostel and a spot of gossip over lunch. Sam is one of the few people who knows about the bender project but then Sam knows everything that goes on around here and she's got the sense to keep her mouth shut about the bits that really matter. If I smelled unduly of mink that day, she was not about to mention it – to me or to anyone else. She gave me soup and made me dry my hair and closed the place for half an hour so she could give me a lift back to the edge of the forest. I didn't need any of these things but Sam has an over-developed maternal instinct that a lover and three kids have never quite diminished and it doesn't do to turn her down.

I watched there every evening after that and we got through to April before it all fell apart. I was there one evening, in my regular watch place: a beautiful horizontal oak limb made all the better with a wee bit of bracken and a handful or two of moss. It was my hideaway, my secret den: the perfect vantage point from which to view an entirely un-perfect crime. The manager left the way he left the first day I was there, ear glued to the mobile, eyes on the clipboard, reversing the monster car without bothering to look in the mirror, without bothering to lock the gate. I should have said something about the gate, I really should. Or perhaps I should have done something more heroic to stop them. But I was too much afraid: six of them to one of me is not good odds and the truth of it is, I couldn't believe anyone could be quite so incredibly stupid. Paint on cars is one thing. Banners. T-shirts. But not this.

It was carnage. You have seen it on the box, you have read of it in the papers but you have no idea, none at all, what it was really like. A tidal wave of frantic, chittering livestock, red in tooth and claw, sweeping out over the land. If I had been on ground level when they first came out, I would be dead by now. They knew that, the ones that did this. They made sure they were high off the ground when they opened the cages and they didn't come down till the flood was over and the ground around the cages was clear. By then, the killing had started. Forget the ones you saw on the box, they are not the deaths that matter. It's the lives you never see that keep this land as it is. The rabbits may be a foreign import, but they are food on feet for everything else that lives and grows. Fox, badger, buzzard, weasel and stoat. Further north, the eagle, further west the harrier and the kite. All of these need the rabbit. The kestrel needs the vole, the merlin needs the wren, the sparrowhawk needs the voles as much as it needs the sparrows. At night, the owls; tawny, barn, little, the long-eared and the short. They all live, breed and rear their young on the small things that live on this land. And all of them, that night, were condemned to the long, slow death of hunger.

We did our best. They had no idea where I came from or who I was but they were glad that I had raised the alarm and they needed all the help they could get. The beasts themselves were hunting, at first, for bits of horse in a dish, not for voles in their tunnels, and they were quite used to wire so collecting them in cages was no hardship to either side. It was when the ones that were out got a taste for killing that things went really bad. You'll lose kids to these things if you're not careful. They're not fussy, not fussy at all about what they eat. I saw nine of them take on an old sow badger. Nine. And it could have been nineteen or ninety for all the difference it made. She fought well and she fought bravely but they ripped her apart. Ripped out her heart and her guts, her eyes and her ears and when it was over there were two of them dead but I didn't see the others stop to count the cost. The whole forest floor was a heaving, sibilant mass by the time I left.

I gave up on the bender that night – you'd have to be more than a little mad to live in a tent with a few hundred mink dropping in to check if there's meat to be had – and went to the hostel to cadge a bed from Sarah and Sam. We watched it all on morning television. You will remember that: the grinning git with no idea of the real world who stood in front of the camera and said that it made no difference what they killed, that if one mink knew one single night of freedom, it was worth any price. It was then that I knew they'd be back.

They came last night and I was waiting. Waiting and watching and following. I did not help catch the new tide last night, I had better things to do. He lives in his own house, the one with the ideas on freedom and its cost. He has a wife and a child, a young child, just about bite-size for a dozen mink. Which is handy really, because I have them with me, chattering softly in the back of the van. You don't need to know how I got hold of the van. Call it a loan. I will replace it in the morning and I promise you will never know. So we are waiting now, my mink and me, for the lights to go out in that house. The git was happy in his work. He knew it is worth any price. He wanted his mink to have freedom and I see no reason at all why they shouldn't be free in his home as much as they have been free in mine. It will be quick, I promise you. One child for the young of all the land. Perhaps after that he will know the cost of freedom. There is always hope.

Ali Smith was born in Inverness in 1962 and lives in Cambridge. Her most recent publication is Other Stories and other stories, *published by Granta in 1999. Her novel,* Like, *was published by Virago in 1997 and her first collection of stories,* Free Love, *by Virago in 1995.*

Kasia's Mother's Mother's Story

By Ali Smith

The woman is making the sign of the cross. Forehead, chest, left shoulder, right shoulder. She does it again, faster, several times. Her right hand flaps in front of her like a small wing or the head of a snake. Anyone watching will think she is making the sign of the cross.

She is standing in the doorway in the early morning dark. Someone passes and she looks down. A bicycle rattles past without slowing. The noise of it dies away. Her shoes are still covered in mud. She will never be able to clean it off them. At some point she will need to find a new pair.

'But we don't need much,' she has been telling her children, combing their hair down with her fingers. 'We need light. We need air. We need

food and water, and to be honest we can do with less of all of these if
necessary. And just at this particular time in our lives, we need prayer.
What do we need?'

'Prayer,' they both say, the tall one and the small one, good like she
wants them to be.

'Say the prayers for me,' she says. 'Out loud. That's good. That's very
good, my good brave girls. Well done.'

Through the nights, through the woods, through the dirt, along the
vanishing track in the dark, shifting the smaller one from arm to arm and
hauling the other by the hand, she said as loud as she dared and over and
over so it became part of the rhythm of the way they moved, the words of
the prayers she wants her girls to be able to say. 'Our Father, who art in
heaven, Hallowed be thy name. Hail Mary, full of grace, the Lord is with
thee, Blessed art thou among women. Come on, say it.'

The street is empty again. She crosses the road. They will be safe enough
in the room until she gets back, and they have been taught not to speak,
and not to say anything to the people downstairs but to be polite, to look
friendly and say nothing. The woman downstairs smiled and nodded when
she was cleaning her doorway. That means nothing. The door is wedged
shut with paper. They are probably still asleep. They will probably still be
asleep when she gets back. It will probably be all right. Her shoes are too
muddy for the town. She will have to find a way of getting them clean. But
it's so early. No one will see.

It is Autumn and the air smells of rotting. The whole town smells of it, a
smell that doesn't go away; it makes no difference where you are in the
town this side of the river or the other. Here the houses are bigger and the
streets are wider. You could look around you and think nothing was
wrong. The shops look as if they might have things worth selling. That
smell at the back of the rotting might even be the smell of a bakery. She
stops in front of the church and tries the door. The handle turns but the
door won't open.

After she has checked for a back door, and tried the side door built into
the wall, she comes back round the front and crosses the road again. This
doorway belongs to a dentist. By the church there, there's a bookshop with
a metal grille over the window.

'Here,' her father says to her inside her head.

It's Summer, it is a beautiful day, it is her birthday. He has a green book on his desk, he is smiling, and he tosses the book across the room with its pages flown open; she catches it against her chest. Stories of Chekhov, bound in green. Down the field by the river there is a good place for reading, a place not too shady and not too hot. Light from the water shimmers the pages. Grass bends by her head. If she just craned her neck she could have the tip of that stem between her lips, in her teeth, she's got it, and she holds the seeds on the end of the stem feeling the rough edges of them against her tongue, and if she is gentle, and careful in the way she moves, and hardly moves at all, she can let the stem go, let it swing back above her forehead and none of the seeds will have broken off.

Stories of Chekhov. She wonders where that book is now. If it is still on the shelf in the back room by the clock that belonged to her mother's mother. If anything is still in its place, where it was left. Who is in the house now. Who has stolen out of it. What things they have taken. She opens her eyes and sees three people going into the church and the door left a little open, and a little open is all she needs.

The dirty walls of the church must once have been white. It smells of damp. It is all long wood seats. She sits on the one nearest the back. The wood is cold through her coat beneath the backs of her legs. There are pictures on the walls. There are statues, and there is a cross at the front: it's too big. A smaller one, a golden one on the table in the middle at the front, looks too expensive. There is a side place with a rail for people to kneel and another statue with another cross. The nun goes past and looks at her. Panic clamps her heart. But the nun doesn't stop. It is all right.

The people are all women, all grim-faced as they go further into the church. She makes her face grim, though her head is lowered, her eyes behind her hair. The priest is dressed in green and white. He stands at the front and raises his arms. They stand up. She stands up.

Forehead. Chest. Left shoulder. Right shoulder.

When they speak she moves her lips. There is no one near enough to hear what she isn't saying. When they change position she does what they do. She blesses the black back of the woman several benches in front, who is so old that she moves very slowly, with plenty of warning, from kneeling to standing to kneeling. When they get up and file down to the front she stays where she is, on her knees, with her face behind her hands. She prays very hard. She keeps her eyes shut.

Now there is the smell of something else, smoke. Someone has put out a

candle and the smell drifts through the church. Some people think it is
enough to bury who you are, to seal it in metal and put it in the ground
and remember where it is. This is too dangerous, she knows, so she burned
their papers when it was light enough for the flame not to be noticed. She
lit the corners one after the other and watched as they blackened and the
blackened pieces broke and blew away, and she stamped what was left into
the moss. She burned her own first and then the girls' and then her
husband's. Before she did this for him she ripped into the parchment with
her teeth and with care, with her cold hands, she tore a ragged path round
his name. She put his torn-out name in her mouth and let the old ink,
dried for years and all of them his, season after season of him, dissolve into
her tongue. She bent down to rub her hands on wet grass to get the ash off
them because soon they would be at the town. Her children sat serious,
waiting shivering on a log. She smiled. Come on then, she said.

'You. Are you all right? Are you unwell?'

Her heart fills with blood. She opens her eyes. The mass is over. There is
nobody left in the church but when she turns she sees the nun standing far
away at the end of the long seat.

'Are you unwell?' the nun says again.

'No,' she says, 'thank you. I'm quite well, thank you.'

'You look unwell.' the nun says. 'Sit down. Do you need a drink of
water?'

'No, thank you,' she says. 'I'm perfectly fine. Please don't bother.'

'Stay there,' the nun says, still looking at her shoes. 'Don't move,' she
says. 'I'll get you a cup of water.'

The nun is gone with the sweeping sound of her clothes. Now all the
woman can hear is her own heart. She slides along the seat, opens the
buttons of her coat as she moves between the benches, and she leans across
the rail at the side, where the robed statue of the lady, its face a little
chipped and its eyes lowered, gazes down at the smaller of the crucifixes.
The cross is made of wood, it will be light, and it is not too big. She picks it
up.

She is over the road with the arms of it pressing into her ribs under her
coat, and as she turns on to the bridge, holding it tight to her side with her
elbow and slowing herself now, so nobody will think she is going too fast,
she imagines the nun coming back with the cup. She imagines her staring
at the side rail, knowing something is wrong.

She imagines her angry face, her arms waving in the air as she calls the priest, who comes hurrying through, and tells him, and tells him what she's done, what she looks like, what she is wearing, exactly what her hair is like, her nose is like, what colour her eyes are.

She imagines the priest telling the grey-black blur of men, with the nun standing humbly by. She imagines the sound of a swerving car, the footsteps quickening behind her.

Slowly. Walk more slowly.

She thinks of the nun, standing holding the cup of water in the empty church. She imagines the silence round her head like the hollow clanging of bells.

She imagines the nun saying nothing, not saying a word.

When she gets back, they are still asleep. They are exhausted. Soon they will wake up and be hungry. She puts the cross on the mantelpiece in the bare-walled room and sits down at the table. She gets up and moves the cross from the middle to the end, where it can be seen from the door. She sits down again. She puts her head in her hands.

It will help, it will help, it will surely help, it will surely do some good. In fact, it is helping already. Now it will be easier to leave them here while she goes to find something to eat.

Raymond Soltysek was born in Barrhead. He has been writing since 1992; since then a few of his short stories have appeared in Scottish anthologies and literary magazines.

Business

By Raymond Soltysek

I never meant what happened.

I just stopped because of the lustre jug in the front room window, blue and white-patterned it was. I saw it through the curtains and thought it might be worth something and business has been slow in the shop, an antique shop; used to be my father's but he died last year and what with the recession no one's buying anything.

I have to keep my eye out.

For good bargains.

Look, I'm not like the sleaze merchants, the ones that spend all day long targeting the sheltered housing – you know, using a penny stall figurine to get in the door and then pay a tenth to clear out all the best items. Like that bastard Davidson, he once got an old Covenanters' chest complete with documented history for forty quid when it was worth at least five hundred, or maybe six. It's not my fault, it's just dead easy to get through the front door. All you do is appear interested in the story, not the jug, like, 'I couldn't help noticing you have one. My mother had one too, but I broke it packing when she died. I thought you could only get them in England – could you tell me where you got it? Oh, you are English – how interesting.'

And that's you in.

See, 'cause old people love telling their stories. It doesn't matter what they part with; if you give them a chance to relive a bit of their lives they'll sell their granny's heirloom for a song, often do. In fact, one old woman gave me her granny's heirloom so that *she* could sing and I listened to some old song about somebody called Barbara and unrequited love and red roses and briars and I said 'How sweet' as I went out the door with two hundred quid's worth of silver teapot under my arm just for listening intently and eating a fig roll with a cup of Earl Grey.

So anyway, there I am and I should give it my all because the old guy's got some really nice stuff, especially some Meissen and a writing desk that must be early nineteenth-century or older if I can get a good look. But 'Yes,' he says, his father bought the jug eighty-three years ago and even then it was expensive, 'Oh, four guineas perhaps' and I'm nodding but not really there, like, which isn't like me if I'm on the scent.

And then that dog of his, stupid-looking poodle, starts yapping – squealing more – at me, as if I'm paying any attention to it. I couldn't give a shit and it scuttles under the table – which I've got my eye on too because it's a really spectacular mahogany – and the old guy's quite upset, 'Trixie's never like this,' he says, and she's such good company since his wife died and when he talks his false teeth rattle around, and he gets down on his knees, clicking his tongue and leaning under the table to encourage the dog out.

Well, I don't know why. I just suddenly felt so tired. I didn't feel violent or any hatred – Christ, I didn't even know him – but just the heat getting to me and the dust smelling musty like old folk and looking down at him on all fours like a dog and hearing that poodle just yapping away . . . I reached down and grabbed his belt at the back of his trousers and he was surprised and went to say something and I caught hold of his collar, greasy with Brylcreem, and yanked his head up. Of course, he was half-way under the table and the back of his head cracked against the underside and there was this thud and a splintering sound and he groaned and went heavy.

I let him go and he sort of crumpled and I looked at him and he seemed like a bagful of washing for the laundry. I couldn't do anything, I mean he was dead so there wasn't any point crying over spilt milk. I took a look around and he really had some nice stuff, even a couple of watercolours worth a few hundred and a writing case he kept under his bed for some reason that had some brilliant inlay. There were some old dresses in the wardrobe – probably his wife's – particularly this black satin one that had thin shoulder straps and sequins and a skirt that flared out; any female would look a doll in it. I even had a look through his kitchen press and right at the back on the floor under the shelves he had this chest of old tools. He must have been a carpenter because they were that kind of gear – planes and wood chisels and things – and they were all pristine like he'd not wanted to get rid of them and spent years polishing them up and treasuring them. Yeah, his own personal treasure chest, that's what it felt like.

For a while it was dead quiet like the only sound was this grandfather clock ticking and a game show went on in a flat upstairs, but then I heard this slurping and then a weird noise like someone hauling themselves upstairs when it's really an effort for them. I went back to the front room and the old bastard was still alive, must have been really tough, a real man's old man as my mother would have said. He was sitting there holding his head in his hands and there was this wound over his ear like a flap of skin had been peeled back and underneath was white like milk. There wasn't much blood, just a few like big pinpricks which looked even more disgusting I reckoned, and his wee dog was licking his chin, standing up on its back legs, its front paws on his chest; it must have woken him, brought him round licking his face, and he looked at me, stupid, like he'd just woken up after sleeping really late. His eyes were staring and blank and his mouth was open and I noticed his teeth were out lying under the table, must have fallen when he hit his head.

I couldn't let this go on, I mean he was really suffering.

And everything was going so well.

I remembered a hammer in the tool chest, a really nice one with a lovely dark wood handle and a heavy claw, so I went and got it and came back and the old guy still just looked at me holding his head and he trusted me, I mean he looked at me as if I could help him even though he didn't know what the matter was, even when I lifted the hammer.

And I couldn't do it, him sitting there like a kid with his wee dog in his lap and I had this feeling of panic for a second, like what the fuck was I going to do now, but somebody up there must like me because he sighed, let out this one long deep breath that came from God knows where and he lay down, keeled over but gentle like, lay his head against the wooden foot of the table leg and just died. I was sure this time because nobody breathes out like that, and the pinpricks of blood began to gather and seep into his hair and this tiny pool appeared underneath his head, staining the carpet. His wee dog whimpered and I kicked it in the rib cage really hard so that it wouldn't interfere. It went bowling into the corner of the room and I brought my heel down on its head, just once though.

It shut up then.

Anyway, I went about my business, what I'd come here for, although things had turned out a bit different from what I'd planned, and I got a couple of pillowcases for the small stuff like the writing case and a couple of bits of Meissen. I wrapped them in old shirts and I took the dress, although I couldn't sell that anywhere, but I liked it, I'd imagine someone in it, someone I'd really want to be with because it's pretty. I found his keys; I didn't know if I'd be able to come back later for the bigger stuff but it was worth thinking about, all depended on how quickly I could move once I'd left, but I did feel that this was all mine, not a power kick like but just that I'd inherited it, that someone was going to have it, so why not me? Then I thought about taking the tools 'cause there's actually quite a market for old craft stuff and I took a look in the chest. Then I remembered the hammer and went back to the living room because I'd put it on the table while I was seeing to the dog and I suddenly wondered about the hammer and the handle and fingerprints so I wiped it carefully on the tablecloth, really did it thoroughly, but I was worried so I took it to the kitchen sink and washed it. Then, of course, I started worrying about the washing-up liquid bottle so I wiped that and all round the sink. Where else did I touch? I thought, dead stupid of me but I couldn't be sure; the wardrobe door, the table edge, the shelves in the press – I even wiped the leather belt around the old guy's trousers. It took me ages to fix but in the end I felt satisfied I'd got it all.

And then the other worries started, really crazy things like how much they could tell and I went down on my knees at the doormat to make sure the imprint of my shoe wasn't there and I inspected the dog's head just in case there was a tread mark that would give me away – my head started aching with it all but I had to be sure and I got the vacuum cleaner out and hoovered the place, walking backwards all the time to pick up after me as I went all the way to the kitchen press where it was kept, and I was going to take my shoes off but then I thought about the fibres in my socks getting into the carpet. Then I had an idea and I took them off and slipped a couple of plastic carrier bags over my feet because I could walk about the place safely and then take them with me and after I'd done that I should have felt safe because I'd decided I wasn't coming back and Jesus I realised I couldn't take anything, absolutely fuck all, and I just dumped the pillowcases on the bed and did a final check to get the fuck out, but things kept swirling about in my head – I couldn't stop them – and it was getting so late 'cause I could hear the ice-cream van jingling down the street and the sun was dead low, orange like, coming in through the front room window showing up the dust drifting around the room, and I remembered someone saying once that dust was just dead skin from people and how far they've got with that DNA business and how much of this was me and I just sank on to my knees to think what I could do about it and it just

wasn't

fucking

fair.

David Stenhouse lives in Edinburgh, where he works as a broadcaster and journalist. He is currently Senior Producer in charge of BBC Scotland's arts programme, 'The Brian Morton Show'.

My Life in Movies

By David Stenhouse

It's thirty years since I first came to the city. Now of course I know it well, but when I first arrived I walked up the hill from the railroad station with my bag in my hand, and had no idea where to go. I'd like to say that I stood and looked across the freeways and the hotel blocks and thought something fine and inspiring – I sometimes tell the story that way – but in fact I had no thoughts in my head at all. Then my body thought for me. There is a word for that. Some guru told me. As we get old all our thoughts get confined in our heads and the brain is the only part of the body that thinks. When we're young our whole body thinks for us. The arms and legs think 'I want to flex, I want to be strong.' The chest thinks 'I want to breathe.' Even the penis thinks.

People are surprised to know I had a life before Marina, but I had. Not a glamorous life certainly, but my own family and friends thought highly of me. Though people in this city never understand it, I was the hero of my small town. I went all the way through school without getting a girl pregnant, without wrapping my car around a tree on the way to a party, without drinking myself unconscious or falling into the same job my father had. And when I ended up in the local paper, on her arm . . . well, that little black and white photo flew across country to me, sent by my aunts, my cousins, kids I'd been to high school with, people I hadn't seen for years. Hundred of copies, falling like snow towards my new life. I had really made it then. First I had escaped, which made me kind of real, and here my reality was confirmed by an airbrushed photograph of her looking radiant, stepping out on the way to an awards dinner with me clutching at her arm. In fact we had argued in the limo on the way to that photo being taken, and only her star's sixth sense had allowed her to compose her features in the second before the bulb flamed up. My face looks odd in that photo, you can't tell what I'm thinking, but in fact I'm half-way between two faces, reacting too late to the flash, and trying to change my expression too. My mother wrote me that the door of every refrigerator in town bore that photograph and its headline, in eighteen point, the one they used for announcing Wars and Crop Failures, 'LOCAL BOY AT OSCARS'.

For most people my life began on 17 May 1969 when I was working in the Fairview Hotel. You'll have heard this story, but let me tell it to you straight. I wasn't stuck there, I was working while I developed my connections in the world of acting. I'd had a few roles, nothing big, but I was getting a name, and I knew my way around the sound stages. Only the week before I'd made an advert, and my agent saw great things ahead for me. That night I was working in the hotel, minding the desk, taking calls, helping the guests check in. It was a quiet night, I remember, and cool; they'd turned the fans off and some of the ladies had slipped on their shawls. Around ten this call comes in from upstairs. The light blinks on a little panel under the lip of the desk, so I know it's a call from one of the special suites. I'd come on at five and there were always celebrities there, so no one had told me to expect anything special. I didn't take the message. That honour went to Jack, who had this very fine voice and so he took the call, and I could see him writing down the order and nodding to himself. 'That'll be coming right up ma'am,' he said. And then he turned to me and said, 'This one is for you' and he smiled this big open smile. Since it was a quiet night I was glad to have something to do.

I got the order from the kitchen and from the bar, nothing too fancy, champagne and this little plate of pastries they did then and I carried them over the hall to the elevators. There was a special elevator for the suites, wood-lined, you needed a special key. I had taken the key out of my pocket already, so I got it into the hole and turned it, but it wouldn't go far enough. It was awkward, balancing the tray on my hand and turning the key, but I forced it a little and it turned. The elevator took off smoothly and gently lifted me the thirty floors to the penthouse.

The elevator arrived and I let myself out. There was this little hall before you got to the suite and I put the tray down and rearranged the flowers on it since they had got a little flat on the trip. Then I tap on the wooden wall before going in. There was no answer. 'Room Service,' I say, looking down at the card on the tray. 'Room Service, Miss Dawn.' Then from the recesses of the suite there comes this incredible voice, soft, low. 'Take it in, boy.'

So I take in the tray and place it on the low table beside the fireplace. I rearrange the flowers again, and place the champagne and the bucket on a small silver stand, and I'm waiting there to see if that will be all.

Then she came out of the bathroom. She had taken a bath and was looking a little damp in her white towelling dressing robe. I point to the tray and ask her if there is anything else she wants. She just looks at me and walks over to her balcony. That hotel did have a fine view over the city, especially so far up. She asked me to come over to the window.

'I don't know this city so well,' she said. 'I've lived here for ten years and there are so many landmarks I don't know. Will you show me?'

The whole city was splayed out at our feet, all the buildings alight like ours, and the cars were zipping along the streets, all lit up. I pointed out to the Mullholland Drive and the Hills. From where we stood we could just see the roofs of some of the studio buildings. As I pointed them out she rested against me a little. I could feel the pressure as she leant on my side. Then she turned to me and said, 'Open that champagne.'

We were always taught to open the bottle carefully in that hotel, wrap the neck in linen, then ease out the cork with your thumbs, but that night something made me turn the bottle towards the window. It took a little pressure but when it came free, the cork shot out over the balcony, driven by a glittering, bubbling stream of white. I could see its trajectory as it flew out over the city, heading towards the Hollywood Hills. She laughed. And I told her that laughing suited her.

We spent the rest of that night just talking. When the desk called for me she told them to give me the rest of the night off. I never found out till it was nearly morning who she was. It was crazy, a big star like her left alone in the city. No one from the studio to look after her. No wonder she was lonely. No wonder she wanted to talk. And what a lot she had to talk about. Her films, her travels. The famous men who had tried to make love to her. 'Phoneys,' she'd say. 'All phoneys.'

The next morning when I went down to the reception no one there would look me in the eye, but I didn't care. By then I knew I wouldn't be working in the hotel for ever.

I moved into her house a week later, and boy what a big lonely place that was. A marble swimming pool, more bedrooms and bathrooms than I'd ever seen before. In the garage there were seven Bentleys. When I first saw them I thought they were all the same, but the chauffeur just swung open the garage doors and in the light I could see they were different. Seven cars, all a different shade of pearl grey. And there were paintings on all the walls. Sculptures everywhere. Outside the rose bushes were arranged in lines, shaped, crimped and pruned. One day she called me up to a room I'd never been in before, just this tiny room at the very tip of the house. There was a little window there and if you looked down from it across the grounds you could see that the bushes spelled out her name. MARINA they said, in green letters. And she was the only one who went up there, so she was the only one who ever saw it.

Sometimes I'd lose her, I honestly would. I'd be walking through the corridor thinking, 'What room were we just in?' And I'd finally find the sitting room where we'd been, but she wouldn't be in it. So I'd sit on the Arabic bed and wait for her to come back. After a while she'd storm in. 'You dummy!' she'd scream. 'We were in the peach sitting room.' And I'd be in the pink, or something.

We had a swell life at first. She was still working then and sometimes she'd be away for weeks on end. Then I'd get a call, in the middle of the night, saying she wanted to see me, and I'd fly into Nevada, or wherever it was and see her. It was always a desert they were shooting in. Always some desert or other. The trucks would come in and they'd kick up a hell of a dust cloud and I'd walk in out of that dust cloud into her trailer. She could have been there for days not speaking but when I arrived I always cheered her up. Sometimes it took a few days, but she always got herself going again. Lately I read in the paper about some producer saying I used to hold up the shooting but what they didn't realise was I was saving their film. When she was unhappy I was the only one who could make her laugh again. Simple as that.

Our life wasn't always easy, though. I didn't realise then that the photographers would be everywhere. Often we didn't leave the house for days at an end. And when I did go out with her there were all these questions. Who was I? Where had I come from? She didn't answer them, of course, just smiled as the cameras flashed. Sometimes those photos made her cry. No one could deny the age difference, and sometimes when she saw the photographers they'd make her mad.

Then came *Wings in the Desert*. It wasn't good from the start. She'd had this thing with the director, Preninger. That was years before but he still felt sore about it. And she didn't like the art director, so things were tense on set. Then she tore a reel out of a movie camera, threw it around screaming that they were lighting her wrong, to make her look old. That she couldn't trust anyone. Refused to come out of her trailer and I was the only one that could reassure her. More dust clouds, more tears. They finally sacked her, but I persuaded her to go back. She shot the rest of that film in two weeks, which is good, even for a young actress.

Then all the legal stuff started. She had a family, though she didn't see them too often. When I'd arrived they hadn't seemed concerned, but when it looked like I might actually *stay*, well, then the letters started coming and then the lawyers started coming too.

I remember one day, they were pressuring her, trying to make her sign her money into trust funds, trying to lock everything up so only the lawyers could get it. It was a day sent from heaven. The pool was aqua blue, as I swam up and down. The sun through the leaves of the trees dappled the water. She was sitting in a lounger, surrounded by lawyers yapping at her, arguing about money and assets. I got up from the water and crept around. They were so intent on bullying her that they didn't see me. Then I grabbed her by the hand and pulled her out of her lounger and into the pool. Water everywhere. All the lawyers were soaked. She sent them away after that. She was laughing. We sure were in love then.

Her film work was drying up, though. *Wings in the Desert* was her last big movie, though she didn't know so at the time. She started getting offers for TV movies, mini-series, invitations to chat shows. She turned them all down, but her agent was on to her to keep her profile up, and then someone persuaded her to go on Merv Griffin that time. She took hours getting made up. I was watching her from the wings. She comes on, big applause and Merv runs through a few jokes and stuff. Then she's in the middle of one of her stories about Cary Grant and how he paid court to her and Merv says, 'Hey, but you've still got that magic now, haven't you?' And she smiles and says she doesn't know what he can mean. And he says 'Well, that young fella that's waiting for you now in the wings. Can we have the picture? Let's have the picture.' And then up on the monitor is a photograph of me and her. I couldn't place it at first, but then I knew. We'd been out to play tennis then we were going on for lunch. It was a hot day and we were having a row. She was tired after tennis, and this guy just pops out from behind a tree to take her photograph and for once it's me that sees it coming, so I smile right into the camera. And this is the photograph they're showing on the Merv Griffin show. It comes up on all the monitors, and the audience in the studio can see it and the audience at home can see it. In this photo she looks about a hundred and I'm standing next to her with this big dumb expression on my face and it looks so strange that I'm with her that Merv's laughing and the audience is cheering and the camera cuts back to her and she's smiling too, but her eyes are shooting hate rays at Merv. When she came off she was screaming at him, and then she was screaming at the director, and then she started screaming at me. That was the last chat show she did.

It was soon after that she got ill for the first time. She'd always been proud of how healthy she was. Used to stand in front of the mirror and say, 'I have the body of a nineteen-year-old.' But one day she fell beside the pool. She lay there for about half an hour before the pool-boy found her. Then tests, hospitals, clinics. She was never really well after that. It was her body not her mind. She was old, yes, but she could never get used to it. Her body was giving up on her, it had stopped thinking, and all her thoughts went round and round in her brain. The doctors said that she needed medication and I authorised them to give it to her.

After she came back from the clinic she needed a lot of help. A lot of the staff had been with her forever but they had to go. They were for serving cocktails at parties, not giving out drugs. I had to make them leave all on the same day and I stood at the front gate and watched them all walking down the hill, looking for buses to take them away. The nurses came in relays, and they were changed often. I got a new guard on the gate and he checked them in and he checked them out. Because she could trust no one I started cooking for her. For two years I cooked every meal she ate. No red meat, lots of boiled fish and chicken, fresh vegetables, and besides that little cups, little clear plastic cups and they'd be filled to overflowing with all her drugs.

Soon after, we moved into the Hawaii house. The climate suited her better, though she wasn't getting well again. She couldn't sleep, so I tried not to disturb her by getting in too early. It was a long summer that year. At first at the parties everyone just knew me through her, but I'm naturally outgoing so before long they knew me as myself. Those beach parties went on late and the scent from the flowers was so powerful some nights it was almost overpowering. I'd walk along the beaches and the waves would be coming in and lapping at my feet and the scent would be coming over in waves too. Often when I got back at three or four in the morning she'd be sitting up pale, exhausted but wide awake, watching the door, waiting for me to come back. She didn't say much but I knew what she was thinking, and I'd lie there beside her until she fell asleep.

Her health did not improve. Two years ago she lapsed into the state she's in now. It was clear that she needed me more than ever.

It wasn't long before the vultures gathered. All these lawyers came out of the woodwork. Safeguarding the monies, securing the position of the relatives, ensuring that there was no unauthorised access to the estate. All that small print made my head ache. And the visits. All these lawyers around her bed. I'd sit in the meetings, though they tried to keep me away, and I'd listen. And sooner or later some young lawyer, straightening his glasses would say, 'Miss Dawn, we're just trying to make sure that after you . . . that the *estate* can be secured.' And that would be it. Whenever that word was mentioned she'd kick them out. She'd manage to lift her hand from the bed and she'd look at me and I'd shoo them away. I'd walk them to the front door, and they wouldn't speak to one another till they'd left the premises.

I was in court more often than I was looking after her. Once the court agreed to a request from the family lawyers to freeze the assets and she had to leave St Hubert's Memorial Hospital and go somewhere cheaper. All the

TV cameras were there and they saw her getting bundled on this stretcher and put into this ambulance to be taken to another clinic. Her fans kicked up hell. I went on the television news and said that her family were trying to fleece her, and that all these moves were going to kill her. There was an outcry about that. Somehow the cameras even got into the cheap clinic to film. The doctors reduced her drugs specially and she was all made up on the bed. She wasn't able to say much, but she held on to my hand and just looked at me. I was able to decipher her whispers as 'I love you. I want my family to leave me alone.' Then the camera took some shots of how grungy this place was and I was able to point out some needles just lying in the corridors that they'd missed. After that the family just kind of melted away. And when she signed over the estate to me there was nothing they could do.

It's an odd life we have now, but we try and make the best of it. She lies upstairs all day, but her mind is still active. I can see these expressions in her eyes and I know what she's thinking. Every morning I stand and look across the city and I think something fine and inspiring. Then I answer her letters, or go to the Marina Dawn gallery, where I'm chairman of the board. I take one of the Bentleys, it's important to keep them ticking over. A different shade for every day of the week. A different shade of pearly grey. And the house we bought has this fine view down over the city. In fact one of the spires on the horizon is the Fairview Hotel, where we stood looking over here, almost thirty years ago. People say, 'Oh you've come a long way.' But it's really just across the city. If I half-close my eyes I can see us now standing on that balcony and looking over here. And I've arranged her bed so that she can see it too. So she can see just how far we've come.

And believe me, that's just how she would have wanted it.

Ruth Thomas's first short story collection, Sea Monster Tattoo, was published by Polygon in 1997. It was shortlisted for the Saltire Society First Book Award and the John Llewellyn Rhys Award. Her second collection, The Dance Settee, was due out in November 1999 (also Polygon). She is currently at work on a novel.

Whistling, Singing, Eating Fruit

By Ruth Thomas

In 1935, Ivy's husband gave her a book. It was called *Don't*.

It had a subtitle: *Social Crimes and Domestic Mistakes*.

'Oh,' said Ivy. She wasn't sure how she was supposed to react.

'In jest, my love,' said Leonard.

'I see,' said Ivy.

She read some of it while she was sitting at the breakfast table. *Don't read at the breakfast table*, she read. The sentence sprang out at her, like a reprimand. It was extraordinary. Out of the corner of her eye, she noticed Leonard raising his eyebrows and looking at her.

There were a lot of chapters about what to do in polite society. Advice on good manners when playing golf, when motoring and when at the bridge table. She never did any of those things; they couldn't afford them. Driving a car would have been fun, but the idea of playing golf or bridge depressed her. There was a chapter in the book called 'For Husbands', which was one and a half pages long. The one for 'Wives' was eleven pages.

Don't wear faded or spotted gowns or anything that is not neat and appropriate, said the first sentence in the 'Wives' chapter. *Dress for the pleasure and admiration of your family.*

She looked down at the tired, upturning collars of her dress.

'Am I wearing a neat and appropriate gown?' she asked. But Leonard had started to read his newspaper and he didn't answer.

The next day she went out and bought herself a new dress. It was very neat: blue with buttoned cuffs and a little collar. The skirt of it reached to the middle of her calves. She tried it on in the shop and looked instantly practical, like a Wren. She wore it when Leonard came home from work in the evening.

'How do I look?' she said.

'Eh?' said Leonard.

'I'm wearing a neat and appropriate dress.'

Leonard looked at her. He didn't reply.

After supper she continued reading the book she had borrowed from the library. *Moby Dick.* She had just got to the part where Captain Peleg was saying '*Fiery pit! fiery pit! ye insult me, man; past all natural bearing, ye insult me,*' when Leonard put his head around the door.

'I've invited Mr and Mrs Cramshaw round for dinner tomorrow evening, my love,' he said.

Then he withdrew his head and walked away, down the hallway. Ivy looked up from her book and stared into space. She heard Leonard stop and tap the barometer in the hall. She wondered what the hand had moved to: Set-fair or Change, maybe.

After a while she put a bookmark in her novel and read another paragraph from the 'Wives' section of her *Don't* book.

Don't confine your reading to novels, it said. *How can women hope to maintain their position as intellectual equals of men if their reading is confined to this one branch of literature?*

She looked in a few recipe books the next day and decided on a stew for the Cramshaws. This was a good thing for a hostess to do, because it could be sitting in the oven while she tended to her guests. She could almost pretend that she had a servant working in the kitchen, basting things. When the Cramshaws arrived, she glittered and sparkled. She drank slightly too much wine. She moved her hands a lot while she talked, and the dining room was filled with the scent of 'Nights In Paris'. While they ate the stew she flirted a little with Mr Cramshaw. She noticed Leonard and Mrs Cramshaw glaring at her but she took no notice of them.

'I'm reading a very good novel all about whaling, Mr Cramshaw,' she said.

'That's an unusual book for a woman to read,' said Mr Cramshaw.

Ivy looked down at the carrots in her stew.

'But commendable,' said Mr Cramshaw.

'Commendable?' she said. 'Do you think so?'

'Ivy,' said Leonard, in a snapping little voice, as if he was commanding a Jack Russell to come to heel.

'Commendable,' Ivy said, stabbing a piece of carrot with her fork. She finished her stew before everyone else: behaviour which was not recommended in the *Don't* book. A hostess was supposed to synchronise eating with her guests.

In 1939 she had a baby. He was bonny, noisy and completely bald. She and Leonard decided to call him Barry. A couple of months after he was born, Ivy discovered that Leonard was having an affair with Mrs Cramshaw. It had been going on for months: secret trysts in the clerk's office; little love-notes and guilty lunches together on a park bench near their office. So she packed a suitcase, put Barry in a pram and left to go and live with her mother.

Leonard's affair didn't last long. Mr Cramshaw turned up to work one day and hit him, breaking a front tooth, and suddenly Mrs Cramshaw seemed to love her husband again. She told Leonard that he was at least a real man. Leonard visited Ivy the same evening, with a swollen mouth and a black eye, and carrying a large bunch of roses.

'I'm sorry,' he said. 'It won't happen again.'

Ivy looked at him, standing on the doorstep with his bunch of flowers.

'I hope not, for your sake,' she said.

'No,' he said. 'I mean – '

'Do you know', she interrupted, 'in that book you gave me, it says *Don't take your love for granted*?'

Leonard's swollen mouth began to quiver and she shut the door.

When the war started, her mother looked after Barry while she went out to work. She had found a job as a park attendant. This involved planting vegetables for the war effort. When the weather was good, her mother would walk to the park with Barry in his pram, and they would sit on a bench and eat sandwiches.

'Do you think you'll ever marry again?' her mother asked her one afternoon.

'Who knows, Mum?' said Ivy. 'If I meet the right man.'

She had already started divorce proceedings. Sometimes she thought of Leonard and wondered how he was getting on. She hoped he was not unhappy. She kept the little *Don't* book on the shelf in her mother's living room, and read it sometimes, when she wanted to be amused and amazed. There was a particular sentence – *Don't whistle, sing or eat fruit in the streets* – that always made her smile.

In 1951, she and Barry moved out of her mother's house into a little flat in Stoke Newington. It had once been part of a terrace, but after all the bombing it had become semi-detached and was quite an imposing sight at the end of the street, standing tall and independent. With her salary and allowance from Leonard, she was able to afford some of the latest household appliances. She bought a twin-tub and a new gas cooker. She also bought a coffee grinder and some wine glasses, and sometimes she invited her friends round for dinner. Most of the time she did things that the *Don't* book scorned: *Don't, when about to give a dinner party, invite more guests than can be accommodated with comfort.* She did this all the time, seating her friends on rickety little chairs and cramming them around the small formica-topped table. She also flirted and made in-appropriately risqué comments.

She met a man in 1962, whom she loved but never married. They just visited each other for twenty-five years, throughout the sixties and seventies and into the eighties. He was her lover, and the *Don't* book didn't even mention lovers. She misses him very much.

She remains in the flat in Stoke Newington, although it is no longer semi-detached; there is an Indian take-away on one side and an Oxfam shop on the other, both of which she finds very useful. Barry, who is now as bald as he was when he was born and works as a washing machine repair

man, comes to visit her twice a week. Sometimes he brings her a bunch of
roses, which reminds her of Leonard. But apart from that, he is not like
Leonard at all.

While they're standing in the kitchen one weekend in October, Ivy asks
him to look at her washing machine, which has stopped working. It just
stopped, she says; in mid-spin.

'Hmm,' says Barry, and he frowns and kneels on the kitchen floor and
tries to pull the machine forward, away from the wall. But he can't manage
it. He's a little too plump and unfit. His face turns rather pink, and after a
couple of minutes he stops trying.

'This is stuck fast,' he says.

'Are you sure, dear?' Ivy asks.

'It's absolutely wedged,' he says.

'Let me try,' she says, and she opens the door of the machine, puts her
hand inside, flat against the steel barrel, and pulls. The machine moves
forward a fraction. She pulls again and it moves a little more.

'How on earth did you manage that?' says Barry.

'Determination,' she says.

She stands up straight and puts her hand on his shoulder. She is
thinking of a little sentence: *Don't undermine a man's abilities. It is more
becoming for women to remain the gentler sex.*

'Ha!' she says.

She is still going strong. She thinks she will make it into the next
millennium.

Copyright acknowledgements

Grateful acknowledgement is made to the following sources for permission to reproduce material in this book previously published elsewhere. Every effort has been made to trace copyright holders, but if any have been inadvertently overlooked the publisher will be pleased to make the necessary arrangement at the first opportunity.

Christopher Brookmyre, 'Bampot Central', from *Fresh Blood 2*, London: The Do-Not Press, 1996 © Christopher Brookmyre

Janice Galloway, 'Someone Had To', from *Where You Find It*, London: Cape, 1997